Double Down

SUSAN HAYES

When it comes to love, sometimes the best bet is to double down.

Kit and Luke Armas are cyborgs created for one purpose, battle. Now that the war is over, they must fight to carve out a place for themselves in a universe they were intended to die for but never be a part of.

Cargo pilot Zura Watson came to the edge of civilized space to start over. The Drift is a haven for the hunted, the lost, and those seeking second chances. It was also the last place in the cosmos Zura expected to find love.

When the shadows of the past threaten to eclipse this trio's future, they'll have to fight for their chance at love and the life they've always dreamed of.

COPYRIGHT

DOUBLE DOWN
Author: Susan Hayes

Copyright © 2016 Susan Hayes
Double Down (Book #1 of the Drift Series)
First Print Publication: July 2016
Cover Design: Melody Simmons ~ ebookindiecovers.com
Editor: Rebecca Cartee ~ Editing by Rebecca
Published by: Black Scroll Publications
ISBN: 978-0-9950950-7-6

DEDICATION

For my parents, Brian and Elizabeth Hayes. I wouldn't be here without your love and constant support. For my best friend in the whole world, Karen, who is always there to help me when my muse pulls a vanishing act.

This book is also dedicated to my readers. You are all simply amazing. Thank you for reading my stories and joining me on my next adventure.

ACKNOWLEDGEMENTS

Thanks to my "J-Team" Julie, Jolanda, and Jenn. I love you ladies; thank you for all your help and support.

Table of Contents

CHAPTER ONE

"Stay the hell out of my bar and away from my staff, or a broken nose will be the least of your problems, asshole." Kit Armas snarled as he tossed yet another drunken idiot out the front doors of his establishment. He watched in silence as the man stumbled away, slurring incoherent threats and curses in a mixture of languages, including Terran, the most common language on Earth, and broken Galactic Standard.

"It's going to be one of those nights, isn't it?" Cyn asked, her tone downright chipper. The tall, rangy brunette had materialized at his side without warning, which was something he knew she did solely to piss him off. She was the only person in the world who could move silently enough to sneak up on him, and she took an unholy joy in doing so.

"It looks that way," Kit agreed as he wiped the latest ejectee's blood from his knuckles with a bar rag.

Cynder Armas was his batch sister and fellow cyborg, as well as his former lieutenant, and now his business partner. Together with his brother, Luke, they owned and ran the Nova Club, which was part fight club, part gambling den, and full-time bar. Kit handled security, Luke managed the bar and kitchen, while Cyn oversaw the staff and handled the finances. Tonight, though, it was all hands on deck, which meant Cyn got to do what she loved most: bust heads. Cynder's primary purpose was stealth and infiltration, not combat, but she loved a good fight. No amount of tinkering had been able to remove *that* glitch in her programming, and the corporation lab-techs had certainly tried.

"Dibs on the next idiot. I've been stuck in the office doing the books for days; I need some play time," she said, cracking her knuckles for emphasis.

"Next one is all yours."

She cheered softly, and Kit rolled his eyes at her.

"You don't have to look so pleased about it, you lunatic."

She flashed him a grin that had sent lesser men running for cover. "It's fight night, the booze is flowing, we've got a full house, and tonight I'm getting paid to kick ass and take names. This is like

Christmas morning for me. At least it would be if you hadn't jumped that guy before I could."

He shrugged. "He went after Teenie when she turned him down for the tenth time. The bastard had it coming, and you weren't there. I was. Besides, the last time I checked, dealing with the rowdies was my job description, not yours."

Cyn scoffed. "We all pitch in for each other, and you know it, especially on a night like tonight. Granted, you probably needed to blow off steam even more than I did. You've been in a foul mood for a week now."

"Have not," he retorted.

"Yep, you have. For oh about…" She made a show of checking her watch. "Seven days, nine hours, and forty minutes. Funny thing, that's the same amount of time that a certain someone's been away on a cargo run."

Kit frowned at Cyn and raised a finger as he ticked off each of his points. "One. I'm not in a foul mood. Two, even if I were, that has nothing to do with anyone's absence. Three. I have no idea who you're referring to. Four. I'm not in a foul *fraxxing* mood."

She laughed and snapped off a salute. "Whatever you say, Major."

"Cut that out. I'm not your Major anymore. What I am is the majority shareholder in this *fraxxing* madhouse we call a club, so quit being a pain in my ass and get back to work."

Cyn stuck out her tongue at him before vanishing back into the bar with the same uncanny speed and stealth with which she had appeared. He had known her his entire life, and he would never get used to the way she did that.

Kit didn't linger at the door himself. Cyn was right; the place was packed tonight, which meant he needed to head inside. It was time to get back to work.

The Nova Club wasn't unique in the Drift. There were dozens of bars, casinos, gambling dens, and pleasure houses scattered across the motley collection of stations and platforms that drifted on the far edge of civilized space, catering to the mining corporations and those who worked for them.

Beyond the Drift was wild space and an asteroid belt full of ore-rich rocks. While they got the occasional exploration vessel passing through, most of the traffic out here was tied to mining. Massive processing ships carried the ore in from the working areas, offloading the refined product onto waiting freighters that shipped it back to civilization. Hundreds of mining vessels worked the asteroid belt, their crews spending months out in deep space before returning. All those crews needed a place to blow off steam and spend their pay, and that's why the Drift had more bars and recreational businesses than it did corporate offices and standard shops.

If there was a way to profit from pleasure, then the corporations had it covered.

The club belonged to Kit and his batch siblings, but they paid a premium to the Astek Mining Corp for the right to run their club. Everything from the space leased, to the liquor and pharma licenses required payments that went straight into Astek's bank accounts. If it weren't for the years of back pay they had been granted when they were finally released from their military contracts, they would never have been able to afford it.

He, Luke, and Cyn were all cyborgs. They hadn't been born, they'd been designed in a lab, grown in maturation tanks, and come to consciousness as adults with a barcode printed on their wrist. They weren't considered people; they were granted no rights or even an identity apart from their alphabetically assigned first names. Cyborgs were nothing more than high-priced commodities, designed to fight in a war that had raged across the starscape for years.

Fifteen years ago, the largest corporations in the galaxy, most of them human-owned, had been at war with each other, fighting for dominance over resources and profits. To win, they needed cannon fodder, but the death tolls were too high for any but the most desperate men to sign up to fight. Desperate men make poor soldiers, so the corporations started making cyborgs to fight their battles for them. Soon, there were no paid soldiers fighting in the Resource Wars at all. There were only the corporations' creations, each one designed to be a perfect soldier. With bodies full of tech, bloodstreams laden with regenerating medi-bots, and minds laden with behavioral programming, cyborgs were a neat, tidy solution to a messy war.

Until the war ended.

Kit and his brethren had fought in the Resource Wars for more than ten years. By the time the fighting was over and the winners had divvied up the spoils, there weren't many of his kind left alive. The corporations had plans to 'humanely decommission' their remaining soldiers, but those plans went to hell when the cyborgs finally revealed their most carefully guarded secret. The ones left alive had long since overcome their programming. They had free will, and they weren't interested in being put down like stray dogs.

In the end, the public outcry had been enough to force the corporations that created them to relinquish ownership. The cyborgs were all freed, their contracts terminated, and each veteran was granted an impressive amount of back pay for all their years of service. By then, there were only three surviving members of Kit's original batch. Luke, Cynder, and himself. They pooled their money and created the Nova Club.

Kit went back inside and began patrolling the club again, looking for trouble in any of its many forms. As he walked, his thoughts kept straying back to the challenges that had brought them out to the Drift. It had taken the collective power of a number of planetary governments to force the corporations to release their creations, but not even that was enough to make people want or accept the cyborgs. It was one thing to rally behind a cause when it didn't affect them, but when Kit and his brethren tried to be part of the civilized world, acceptance proved hard to come by.

Things were easier out here in the Drift, but even so, there were biases to be overcome. Nearly every race and species had an innate distrust of anyone or anything that was different, and cyborgs were something none of the other races were familiar with. Kit and his brethren might look human, but there was enough tech and steel inside his body to ensure there would always be those who thought of them as nothing more than machines. People like Andrea Rankan—the woman who had stomped on his heart.

"Will you quit glowering at everyone? You're putting the customers off their drinks."

Kit's train of thought was derailed by his brother's voice. His patrolling had brought him around to Luke's domain, the bar. He glanced over to the far side of the gleaming chrome countertop to where Luke was standing. The smile on his brother's face didn't quite reach his eyes. Instead, his lips were pursed, and his arms were crossed over his chest, almost completely hiding the blue and silver bar logo emblazoned on his shirt.

"You okay?" Luke asked over their internal comm channel.

"Just thinking," Kit answered aloud. He was in no mood to have his brother's voice in his head.

Luke snagged a bottle from behind him and poured two glasses of something clear that bubbled and smoked as it hit the ice at the bottom of the glass. "I'm not even going to ask who you were thinking about. I know it was Andrea, again."

"What gave it away?"

"The thunderous look on your face. You need to let it go, Kit. She was a cold-hearted bitch wrapped up in a pretty package. There are plenty of other stars in the sky. I wish you'd pick a new one to orbit around."

"Yeah, I know."

"I can already hear the 'but' on the end of that sentence. She screwed us both over, remember? I was there, too. We got burned, but I'm not going to let that stop me from trying again."

Kit eyed the freshly poured drink and decided a change of topic was in order. "What the *fraxx* is that?

Luke pushed one of the glasses toward him. "This is something new."

"Why is it bubbling?" He started to reach for the glass and then froze as the drink slowly changed colors, first to orange, then red. "I'm not drinking that."

Luke laughed. "Relax, it's just a chemical reaction with the ice. If you don't try it, Zura will be very disappointed. She brought this in especially for us."

"There isn't a snowball's chance in a supernova that I'm going to drink—" He stopped as the rest of what Luke had said sunk in. "Wait, the *Sun Sprite* is back already? When? Where is she?"

Zura Watson was the owner and pilot of one of the many freighters that came and went from the Drift. She first appeared at the club six months or so ago, always alone and never saying more than a few words. At first, all she had been was another customer, albeit one of the more pleasant ones. She paid her tab, stayed quiet, and never started trouble. The few times trouble had come looking for her, she had made short work of the ones giving her grief. It didn't take long for word to spread that manhandling the *Sun Sprite*'s pilot was a bad idea unless you had a thing for pain and visits to the medical center.

He hadn't known much about her in the beginning, apart from the fact she kept to herself and always paid her tab. He and Luke had been too busy running the bar and dealing with the fallout of the implosion of their relationship with Andrea to notice much of anything or anyone. That's what he told himself, anyway. Luke's theory was less complimentary and involved Kit having his head up his ass while stubbornly refusing to see what was right in front of him.

All that had changed when the outbreak hit. A lethal virus tore through the Drift, infecting hundreds. Human, Jeskyran, even the normally unstoppable Torskis proved to be vulnerable to the infection. The medi-bots all cyborgs carried in their bloodstream had protected Kit and his brethren, but they'd been some of the lucky few.

Within days, the medical staff was overwhelmed. Then, the emergence of a cosmic storm had added to the crisis. The vaccine they needed was waiting for them light-years away, but the storm made space travel insanely dangerous. Only one pilot volunteered to go: Zura Watson.

She made the run and returned to the Drift with all the vaccine they needed, saving countless lives. Both she and her ship paid the price, though. The *Sun Sprite*'s shield generators were burned out, and her engines had been pushed past their breaking point. As for Zura, flying through the storm had exposed her to dangerous levels of radiation, leaving her so weak, she had barely managed to dock before falling unconscious for days.

Some of the lives Zura had saved belonged to the staff of the Nova. As far as Kit and Luke were concerned, offering her a place to crash while she recovered and her ship was repaired was the least they could do. It had turned out to be the best decision they could have made, because it gave them a chance to get to know her better. She was so much more than either of them had ever imagined.

Even weakened and ill, she had found reasons to joke, and laughter had become a common sound to hear coming out of her room whenever she had a visitor. At first, not many had come by, but as the club staff got to know her, they spent more time there, bringing her meals, games, and bits of gossip to help keep her from getting bored.

Both he and Luke had started spending more and more time in her company, attracted by her wit and good humor as much as her beauty. She was a kind soul wrapped around a core of steel, and as she had slowly recovered, the three of them had become good friends.

Eight days ago. Zura had left on her first run since she had been cleared for flight duty, and Kit had missed her more than he cared to admit.

His brother snickered. "Yeah, she's back. She showed up here about ten minutes ago. She came by to say hello while you were making your rounds and then went looking for a free table. You feel like taking a few minutes off your constant patrolling to say hi?"

"You could have opened with that information and skipped the lecture about Andrea, you know. Hell, you could have sent me a comm message telling me she was here when she arrived."

"And where would be the fun in that? Besides, you needed the reminder. We've talked about this; it's time to move on. Bring your drink and follow me. Last time I saw her, she was headed for the VIP section."

"You're an asshole," he muttered, but he picked up his glass as his brother vaulted the bar to join him.

"We're genetically identical, which means you're one too." He picked up the bottle and his glass off the bar. "Come on, asshole, let's go find our favorite pilot."

Kit's mood lightened at the news that Zura was back. She insisted on flying her ship solo, which was cost-effective, but risky. If anything went wrong, she was on her own. Her job took her to some of the roughest places in the sector, and it bothered him that there was no one watching her back.

He and Luke were more than brothers, they were twins. They had been designed to work as a command team, trained to think and act as one. They were even linked to each other via internal comms, able to communicate and monitor the other's bio-signs. Kit had never been truly alone in his life, and as much as that irritated him sometimes, he couldn't imagine what it would be like to face life the way Zura did, completely on her own, with no one she could rely on.

The thing was, with each passing day, he was feeling more and more like he wanted to be someone she *could* turn to. After swearing off women for life, Kit felt like a fool for even considering going down that path again so soon. Zura was special, though.

There was no doubt that their first attempt at a normal relationship had been a spectacular failure. They wanted a woman to love and share, while it turned out that Andrea was only interested in playing around. She'd done a number on them both, but Luke was ready to move on. He had been waiting for Kit...and it was plain to see that Luke was done waiting. Kit wasn't sure he was ready, but he had promised Luke he would try.

He followed Luke across the club, idly noting that the moment his brother left the bar, another bartender stepped up to fill his spot. It had taken them time to learn what they were doing, but these days the Nova ran smoothly. Everyone here took pride in their job and in the club itself. They weren't merely employees; they were like family.

Luke led the way toward where he had last seen Zura, the bottle of liquor and an empty glass in one hand and his full glass in the other. He knew Kit was only a few steps behind him, no doubt scanning the crowd for potential trouble with every step he took. These days, looking for trouble was all that Kit seemed to do.

Both he and Cyn were worried about Kit. Andrea had broken both their hearts, but Kit didn't seem able to pull himself out of the tailspin she had put him in. He had been in a dark mood ever since she had dropped a plasma bomb into their happy threesome and walked away from the ashes. All he did was patrol the bar or sit at the security station and scan the monitors. The only person who could bring a smile to Kit's face was Zura. When she was around, he was more like his old self, the one who laughed and joked and always had to get the last word.

Luke spotted Zura without any problem, despite the dark atmosphere of the bar. She was seated at her favorite table, the window giving her a view of the ships coming and going from the docking arms outside. She was looking out the window when they approached, but when they neared her table she turned to smile at them.

"You again, Luke? Did you miss me already?"

"Care to join us for a drink? Since you brought this stuff, it seems only fair you get to try it with us," Luke said, holding up the bottle.

He might have seen her less than ten minutes ago, but that didn't stop him from taking a moment to admire her again. She was of mixed species, half human and half Pheran, and he suspected her alien appearance was one of the reasons she kept to herself. Full Pherans looked vaguely feline to human observers, complete with rounded eyes, tufted ears, and stripes that resembled the long extinct tigers of Earth. Zura's appearance was less cat-like, but it was obvious that somewhere in her past, her mixed heritage must have drawn unwanted attention. She hid herself away and always seemed surprised when anyone noticed her.

As far as Luke was concerned, though, she was breathtaking. She had the blue skin of her Pheran mother, with subtle stripes of even deeper blues marking her face and body. Her hair was made up of a myriad of shades of blue, ranging from cerulean to indigo, and her rounded, silver eyes were currently alight with pleasure. As usual, she wore a long, flowing cloak that obscured her body, though tonight she had left the hood down, revealing her face. She had only started doing that in the last few weeks, and Luke took it as a good sign. He wanted her to feel safe at the club and with them.

"I've never said no to a free drink in my life. Take a seat, and we'll give this stuff a test flight. Hey, Kit. Nice to see you taking a break for once."

"Welcome back, Zura. You made good time. I'm assuming that means it was a smooth run." Kit set his drink down and claimed the seat to her right, leaving Luke to claim the seat on her left.

She held out her hand and ran it level to the table top. "Smooth sailing all the way. Even the paperwork was in order for once. I think they were taking it easy on me. Speaking of freight, I talked to an old friend of mine while I was gone. He's one of the colonists on Tagar 9, and he's willing to ship real, grass-fed beef to you guys if you're still interested."

Luke sat down and let out a low whoop of joy. "*Fraxx* yes, we're interested. Our customers would pay premium prices for real beef this far from civilized space. You're amazing, you know that? We've been trying to find a reliable supplier for non-synthetic meat since we started this place. It's been a lost cause until now."

She shrugged. "It's a lot easier to make deals when you've known the people involved for most of your life. My father used to transport Dag's livestock for him when he was still trying to build up his herds. You have no idea how much mess a half-dozen cows can make when they're stuck in a cargo bay for a couple of days. I swear it took a year to get the smell out."

"Having never seen a cow, I can only imagine. I've only ever seen such creatures after they've been reduced to tasty serving-size. Did you really transport live animals? Wouldn't embryos be easier?" Kit asked, curious.

"Embryos take time to mature. Dag spent a small fortune bringing in some fully grown animals to get a head start building up his herd. Have you really never seen a cow?"

"Only in videos and sims," Kit said.

"Not a lot of livestock on the planets we've visited. The wars were predominately fought over uncolonized planets, moons, and asteroid fields. Most of our planetary time was incredibly dull, if you discount the fact someone was usually trying to kill us." Luke said.

"If you ever want to see a cow up close, Tagar 9 isn't that long a trip. I could take you. I hear it's a pretty place, if you like farmland."

"I'm happy right here. I've got no plans to ever visit another planet," Kit said.

"Plans change. If you ever change your mind, I would be happy to let you charter the *Sun Sprite* somewhere. I hear the Horus system is nice this time of year," she offered.

Luke scoffed. "Horus is not my idea of a vacation spot, thank you. That whole system is one *fraxxing* ice planet after another. I would rather go somewhere with sun-drenched beaches, a warm ocean, and someone else serving the drinks for once. For that, I might consider putting up with inconveniences like weather and gravity."

Zura Watson didn't like to admit it, but she had missed the company of the two cyborgs while she had been away. She had always found them attractive. There probably wasn't a female in the Drift who didn't, no matter what species they were. The Armas brothers were both well over six feet tall, with bright blue eyes and dark brown hair. Kit wore his swept back from his face, while Luke's hair was always falling into his eyes, a trait that had Zura's fingers itching to tuck it back in place. Their hair was the only way to tell the two of them apart. They were identical in every other way, right down to the barcodes imprinted on their left wrist.

During her recovery, she had gotten to know the brothers as more than the men who ran her favorite bar in the Drift. Somehow, despite her best intentions to keep to herself, they had become her friends—big, buff, sexy-as-hell friends.

The truth was that the two of them had played a starring role in more than a few of her fantasies the past few months. She knew enough about them to know that they shared *everything*, including the women they took to their bed. That discovery had fueled her fantasies for weeks as she wondered what it would be like to be tangled up with the two of them at once.

Not that she expected them to ever return her interest. They were so far outside her orbit it would be insane to imagine they'd look twice at a half-breed freighter jockey like her. At least, that's what she used to think. Since she had been invited to stay at the Nova to recover, things between them had slowly started heating up.

It was in the way they watched her sometimes when they didn't think she was looking. Small touches and flashes of tenderness that she never saw them show to anyone else. They had been flirting, too, but she knew better than to take that too seriously. They were in the hospitality business; making people feel good was part of the job. Besides, the last thing she needed was entanglements, in the sheets or out of them. She kept reminding herself that she came out here to start over again, not repeat the mistakes of the past.

Kit snagged the bottle from Luke and poured her a glass of the liquor she had gifted them with. "Not me. I have better things to be doing than roaming around a planet getting my boots dirty."

She took the glass and raised it in a toast. "To spending our time on the better things in life. Like sharing a drink with friends."

"To sharing time with good friends," Kit repeated, while Luke merely nodded. They raised their glasses and drank, and three seconds later both males' glasses were empty.

"That's good. Really good. Where'd you get it?" Luke asked.

"You're not going to believe this, but I got it from a mining ship. They're making it themselves."

Kit scowled. "That's homebrew? Are you trying to kill us?"

"They've been drinking it for months. I figured it was safe enough. Besides, Luke ran it through the scanner before he opened it. It's fine, right Luke?"

"Totally. And tasty, too. If you can get them to part with more next time, I'd be happy to stock it."

"I'll see what I can do, and since we're friends, I'll even waive my finder's fee," she joked, taking another sip of her drink.

"How about I create a new cocktail and name it after you as a thank you?" Luke offered as he poured another glass.

"And what would you call it? Zura Juice?" she asked with a laugh.

Luke choked on his drink. "*Fraxx*, no. Give me a little credit, will you? First, I have to figure out what to mix this with, and then I'll work on a name. Creating a new drink is an art-form, best you leave it to the professionals. You stick to piloting that rust bucket of yours."

"Rust bucket? You did not just insult my baby!" she exclaimed, well aware Luke was teasing her.

He threw his big hands up in the air in mocking surrender. "I take it back. She's not rusty. She's gorgeous, just like her owner."

"Better. You know I don't let anyone put down my ship. You didn't have to add in the flattery, though."

"That wasn't flattery, I meant it," Luke said.

Kit leaned forward slightly and gave her a look so intense she forgot to breathe. "You're gorgeous, Zura. Believe me. There isn't another female in this bar that compares to you,"

"Agreed," Luke chimed in.

"Cynder would likely take exception to that statement," she said, as her pulse started to race, and warning alarms went off in the logical part of her brain. This was taking their flirtations to a new level, and damn, she liked it more than was wise.

"Cyn's our sister, she doesn't count," Kit said and shrugged in dismissal.

He seemed about to say something more, but before he could, there was a loud curse and the crash of glass shattering. His head snapped up as he looked for the source of the disturbance.

"Gotta go," he muttered as he rose from the table and headed toward the fight breaking out on the far side of the bar.

She watched as the crowd of patrons parted before him, giving the big cyborg a wide berth. There weren't many beings in existence who would deliberately put themselves in the path of a cyborg on a mission. Whoever had broken the peace, they were about to regret it.

"And there he goes, the master of romance and seduction. Utters one compliment, then wanders off to break up a bar fight," Luke said with a sigh.

"Romance and seduction? Is that what you two are up to?" she asked, trying to keep her tone light despite the sudden pounding of her heart.

Luke winked at her. "If you have to ask, then we haven't been doing a very good job of it."

Her stomach did a slow somersault, and a voice in the back of her head started to cheer wildly. Holy *fraxx*, she hadn't imagined their interest.

Before she could say anything, a loud crash followed by a screech of pain and angry shouting had Luke on his feet in a second.

"*Re'veth*, someone's trying to get themselves killed. Be right back, gorgeous."

He was gone before she could say another word. She marked his passage through the crowd, who moved out of his way with the same speed as when his brother passed through.

The fight was over shortly thereafter, and she caught a glimpse of Kit lugging a barely-standing customer toward the exit. Luke was right behind him with an unconscious patron slung over one shoulder. Neither of the cyborgs had so much as a hair out of place. She took a moment to enjoy the sight of their heavily muscled arms flexing as they hauled the troublemakers across the bar and out of sight.

She knew it would be a while before either of them would be back to finish their drink, if they got the chance to come back at all. The club was nearly full now, and the cage fights would start shortly, which meant the brothers would soon be too busy to socialize…or flirt.

The safe, sane voice in the back of her head was whispering again, reminding her that this wasn't a good idea. She had come out to the Drift to get away from her old life and start over. The smart choice was to keep the brothers at arm's length. The problem with the smart choice was that it meant walking away from two of the sexiest, most decent men she had ever met.

If her father were here, he would remind her of one of his favorite sayings—no risk, no reward. If it meant having a chance to be with Kit and Luke, then she suspected she was willing to risk a hell of a lot.

She downed the rest of her drink and sighed. What the *fraxx* was she going to do? Stay safe and alone, or gamble with her heart and see where things went with Kit and Luke?

CHAPTER TWO

Kit's night wasn't going the way he had planned, not by a long shot. He still couldn't believe he had blurted out that compliment and then walked away from Zura two seconds later to deal with a fight. *Not my finest moment.*

Now, it was like the universe was out to mess with him. Every time he tried to get back to Zura, some new problem cropped up. One of the night's fighters was a no-show and another one was too drunk to stand up on his own, never mind step into the ring. Then club security caught one of the club's licensed pharma dealers selling undocumented product, which meant reporting the infraction to Astek Corp and security. He'd left Cyn to deal with that problem, including filling out the headache-inducing reports that corporate security would require.

He hadn't been able to say a word to his brother, either, and at the moment, Luke looked almost as frustrated as Kit felt. They both wanted to get back to Zura, but the universe wasn't giving them a break.

It was over an hour later before he finally got a moment to himself. He headed straight for Zura's table, and when one of the other security guards stepped in for a word, Kit shook his head and waved the other man off. "I don't want to hear about it. For the next twenty minutes, I'm not available for anything less than an invasion, explosive decompression, or a four-alarm fire. Got it?"

Owen nodded. "I'll handle it."

Kit was halfway to the gaming area before he spotted Zura. She was still seated at the same table, their drinks still sitting where they left them, untouched and waiting for their return. Well, at least she hadn't cut and run on them. After the less than stellar approach he had taken tonight, he wouldn't have blamed her if she had. He wasn't much for romance at the best of times, but even he knew that growling a compliment then bailing wasn't the best approach to take with a woman he was trying to impress.

His pleasure at seeing her again evaporated the second he saw she wasn't alone. There was a Jeskyran sitting across from her, and the newcomer's body language set Kit's teeth on edge. Something wasn't right.

Resisting the urge to charge in, Kit closed the distance slowly as he strained to hear what was being said. He knew he was eavesdropping, but he didn't give a damn about Zura's privacy at the moment. The second he got close enough to see her face, he knew he was right to be concerned. Her silver eyes gleamed with annoyance, and her fingers were strumming the tabletop, a sure sign she was unhappy. Another step, and he was close enough to hear every word.

"You keep saying no like you have a choice in this, Zee. That's not how it is. These days, what Vin wants, he gets. So be smart and say yes before things get...unpleasant."

Zura lifted the fork she was toying with and pointed the prongs at her gaunt and angular companion. "Vin will have to learn to live with disappointment. Whatever he wants to meet with me about, it's not going to happen. For *fraxx* sake, he stole from me and put me in medical for three days. How can he possibly think we have anything to talk about?"

"Zee, you need to think this through. Things have changed back home."

"If you call me that nickname one more time, I will jam this fork somewhere you won't enjoy it, Ganzer. Only my father got away with calling me Zee. Go back to your soulless bastard of a boss and tell him my answer is no."

"You don't know what you're saying, Zee—Zura. You say no, you're going to get hurt…again. I don't want to see that happen."

Kit had heard enough. He was at Zura's table in seconds and planted a hand on the alien's shoulder, though he was careful to place his fingers so they missed the groupings of thorns that rose from his mottled orange and yellow skin. Jeskyran's were an unattractive species, both physically and in personality. It didn't help that because of their thorny skin, they rarely wore more than a loincloth.

"She gave you her answer, asshole. I suggest you accept it and go." In order to make his irritation clear, Kit didn't bother being subtle. Instead, he gripped hard enough to cause the Jeskyran to yelp in pain and surprise.

"Who the *fraxx* do you think you are that you can tell me when I should go—oh, *veth*." The alien's tone changed to one of dread as he twisted around and got his first look at Kit.

"I could have handled him," Zura muttered, but she was grinning as she said it.

"I know you could have, but it's my bar, and you're my guest," Kit said before deliberately grinding his fingers deeper into Ganzer's shoulder joint.

"Okay, okay! I'm going. I'll take your message to Vin, Zura, but he's not going to like it."

Zura's eyes narrowed. "He doesn't have to like it, but he's going to have to accept it. I'm not going back. I've moved on."

Ganzer bolted the second Kit released his grip and didn't look back once on his way out.

"Moved on from what, or who?" Kit asked.

Zura shrugged. "I've made some mistakes in my life. The thorn-covered creep who just left works for one of the biggest errors in judgment."

"You want to tell me about it?" he asked, surprising himself with the offer. Talking wasn't really one of his strong points, but if Zura was in some kind of danger, he wanted to know what it was. He also wanted to hear more about the son of a starbeast who had put her in medical.

"No, I don't. It's really not a big deal."

"If someone's coming into my bar and warning you to do as you're told or else, I'd say it's a bigger deal than you're letting on. I heard you say something about being hurt so badly you wound up in medical. That sounds like a big deal to me. You're our friend. We don't leave friends to fight their battles alone...Zee."

She glared at him. "Don't even think about it. The nickname was my dad's idea. My mother's parents named me, and he hated the name they chose, so he shortened it to Zee. I prefer Zura, though." Zura didn't answer Kit about what Ganzer had wanted. If she started explaining, it would take the rest of the night, and she wasn't ready to share. She was still dealing with the revelation that her ex-boyfriend, Vin Collins had tracked her down. She had fled to the edge of civilized space to get away from the asshole. How much further did she have to go?

Kit nodded. "Okay, Zura. That jackass is banned from the Nova, though."

She laughed at the dark expression on his handsome face. "By all means, ban Ganzer. That'll make it impossible for him to interrupt another of my meals before he heads back to give Vin the bad news. Now that we've got that out of the way, you want to sit down and finish your drink?"

"That was my intention when I came over here. I also wanted to apologize for walking away earlier. Your friend isn't the only one lacking in manners tonight." Kit settled his big frame into the chair across from her and retrieved his glass.

"No need to apologize. This is your place, and you need to keep it running smoothly." She finally realized she was still holding the fork in her hand and set it down on the table, only to pick it up again a second later so she could idly flip it around her fingers.

"Still, it wasn't my finest moment. I could have let someone else deal with it, but I'm not good at delegating." He paused and then scrubbed a hand through his dark hair. "I'm not as smooth as some people, but even I know that complimenting a beautiful woman shouldn't be followed up by walking away before she can even say anything."

"It was a nice compliment, though," she said, smiling a little.

"I meant it. You're beautiful, Zura, and I'm not just saying that to be flattering. When I say something, it's because I mean it."

"I know. It's one of the things I like about you. You just caught me off guard is all. You have to admit, you're not one for compliments."

He grinned a little. "You noticed that, did you? As I may have mentioned, I'm not much for small talk or social niceties. That's really Cyn's skill set. "

"I meant to ask you all about that one day. You're all from the same, uh…batch, right? So why are you and Luke so similar and Cyn's well…Cyn?"

Kit didn't speak for a moment, and she wondered if she had somehow stuck her foot in her mouth.

"You haven't read up on what we are, have you?" he asked softly.

"Not really, no. Somehow that seemed, well, rude. Then again, so is asking such a personal question, so maybe I should have looked it up instead."

"You might not have found the answers anyway. There isn't a lot of information on my kind. The corporations may have been forced to free us, but they still consider our development and designs to be highly classified. Maybe you should tell me what you do know, and I'll try to fill in a few of the blanks," he said.

"I really don't know much. You are human, but with cybernetic parts. Your bones are infused with metals to make them denser and harder to break, and they did something to your muscles, so you're stronger than a normal person. I know there's software involved too, because the corporations thought you were all blindly obedient until you refused to let yourselves be destroyed. That's, it really."

"That covers the basics. We're bigger, stronger, with generally faster reflexes and greater endurance. Everything a soldier needs to be, only without that annoying free-will issue getting in the way. There's more, but that depends on when we were created, and for what purpose. We're all a little different, even if we were made by the same corporation."

"Is that why Cynder doesn't look or act like you and Luke?" she asked.

He nodded. "Luke and I are twinned clones. We're genetically identical. We even shared the same maturation tank. Cyn's a twinned clone, too, but her sister, Dana, died in the wars. Not every cyborg has a twin, but many do. It all depends on what role we were designed to fill and which corporation created us. I've heard about triplets, too. Never met any, though."

"I didn't know about her twin. How long ago?"

"Somedays it feels like we lost her only a few days ago. Other times? It feels like a lifetime."

"I know how that goes," she said, thinking of her dad.

"Your dad, right? I'm sorry."

"It's okay. I don't think about it much, but sometimes it sneaks up on me."

He nodded. "Yeah, it does. Losing family is never easy."

They lapsed into silence, but before she could think of something to say, he started to talk again.

"Technically, Cyn's not really our sister, but she is family. We share some DNA, but that's not why we think of her as a sibling. She was part of the batch Luke and I were well, born with, for want of a better word. There were twenty-four of us in the beginning. We all matured at the same time and were designed to work as a team. Everyone had a role, and we were created to be the best we could be at whatever that role was. Cyn, Luke, and I are all that's left, now."

"You lost everyone else?" Zura's heart ached at the thought of losing so many. One death had nearly destroyed her, she didn't know how Kit and his siblings kept going.

"I didn't know about the batch thing, or that you'd lost all your brothers and sisters. I'm so sorry. I can't imagine."

He shrugged. "It was war. I'm just grateful the three of us made it out and found our way here. The club is more than our business; it's our home. The first one we've ever had."

"I'm glad you made it out, too. The Nova is my favorite place in all the Drift." She paused and then added. "And thanks for allowing me to dodge your earlier question about Ganzer. I'm not ready to talk about it."

Kit nodded, his eyes full of understanding. "I figured. I hope one day, you'll tell me all about it. I want to know the name of the man who hurt you. That way if I ever meet him, I can return the favor."

She was surprised at the dark undertone of his words. It was clear that he meant what he said, every word of it. When the surprise faded, she belatedly realized she hadn't answered him yet. "One day, yes. We can trade stories about our old lives. You and me and Luke."

"I'd like that. The three of us, talking. Maybe over dinner?" he asked.

She blinked. "Dinner?"

"Yeah. You know, that meal that comes at the end of the day? You, me, Luke, food, conversation, maybe even some of the good booze we keep stashed away for personal use."

"Are you asking me out on a date, Kit?" She felt foolish for asking, but she needed to be sure. It would be so much worse if she misunderstood and got her hopes up.

"Yes, I—" Kit stopped midsentence and swung his head around to glower at one of his security guards who appeared out of the darkness that blanketed the bar. "What do you want, Owen?"

"I know what you said before, but uh, the kitchen *is* actually on fire. Well, it was. It's out now, but I thought you'd want to know."

"*Fraxx*! You have got to be kidding me. How the—no, forget it. I'm going to want to hear this for myself." Kit slammed his glass down on the table with another muttered curse before standing up.

"I'm sorry, Zura. It's been one of those nights. You sticking around to watch the fights?"

She pushed the bottle of liquor toward him and shook her head. "I'm headed back to the *Sun Sprite* to catch up on my sleep soon. It's been a long week for me."

She swore he looked disappointed for a moment, but the expression was gone before she could be sure.

"Dinner tomorrow. Please? I swear we won't get interrupted next time," he said.

"Tomorrow," she said with a nod, barely able to contain herself.

"I'm looking forward to it." He let his hand cover hers for a second, then picked up the bottle and headed toward the kitchen.

Holy hell, I have a date with Kit and Luke.

She flagged down a passing waitress and ordered a double-thick chocolate milkshake. She was going to need the sugar rush to deal with the weird twists tonight had brought. In the plus column, she had a date with two amazing men. On the negative side, she had a date, which was not on the Zura-ratified plan for her new life out in the Drift. As an added bonus, there was a second negative. Vin knew where she was, which meant trouble was coming. Why couldn't he just leave her the *fraxx* alone?

* * * *

Luke kept an eye on Zura as he worked. He wished like hell he could have spent more time with her than the brief moment it took to deliver her dessert. She had greeted him with a smile, but there were shadows in her eyes that hadn't been there before. She had something on her mind, and he didn't doubt it had something to do with the unwanted visitor who had been at her table earlier. Kit hadn't been able to spare more than a few minutes, but he had updated Luke on what he had overheard as well as letting him know they had a date with Zura tomorrow night. That last bit of news had made Luke's night.

Zura didn't stay long after she finished her milkshake. She wove her way through the crowd of patrons, coming close enough to the bar to wave at Luke on her way out. He gave her a smile and a wave back, and the moment she was out of sight, he dropped the bar cloth and signaled for one of the other servers to take his place. The conversation with Kit might have been brief, but they both agreed that she wasn't walking back to her ship alone. Since his brother was nowhere to be found, Luke was more than happy to go. It had been a long shift, and a few minutes away from the noise and hectic pace of the bar would be a nice break.

He activated the personal comm channel they shared and let Kit know that Zura was leaving; he would be back once she was safely onboard the *Sun Sprite*. Once that was done, he followed her out the front doors, making sure to leave enough distance between them that she wasn't likely to spot him. Somehow, he didn't think she would be grateful for the escort. She was used to taking care of herself.

The hardest part of following her turned out to be walking slowly enough to stay out of sight. His long-legged stride was nearly equal to two of hers. Not a surprise considering that at six-foot-six, he stood almost a foot taller than her. At five-foot-seven or so, she wasn't exactly short, but compared to himself and Kit, she was tiny.

Once they reached the docking area, he had to fall back even farther. There were only a few corporation personnel around, along with a handful of crewmen belonging to the various ships currently in port.

They were nearly to her docking bay door when Luke spotted two men loitering not far from the *Sun Sprite*'s berth. One look was all it took for him to know they were trouble. They were both unkempt and rough around the edges even by Drift standards, not to mention that neither of them were wearing ID's or uniforms that would indicate what vessel they belonged to. He lengthened his stride, determined to close the distance between himself and Zura. He was no longer worried about her spotting him. He was more concerned about the two men who were watching Zura approach with far too much interest for his liking.

* * * *

Zura was thinking about the events of the night as she walked back to her ship. Her thoughts kept her distracted enough that she didn't notice the two men in the otherwise empty corridor until she was too close to turn back without being spotted. A lifetime spent in the company of rough men, smugglers, and criminals had honed her instincts sufficiently, so that she knew without a doubt the two men were here for her. Apparently, Ganzer's warning hadn't been an idle threat after all. Whatever Vin wanted from her, he wasn't wasting any time.

She briefly contemplated turning back despite being seen; they were close enough that they would most likely come after her anyway. She didn't like having them at her back. Her father had taught her it was always best to face danger straight on. That way, she knew what was coming.

She kept walking and made it most of the way to her ship when the bigger of the two men stepped in to block her path. He jerked a thumb toward the door to the *Sun Sprite*. "That your ship?"

She came to a stop a few feet outside the big man's reach and looked up at him, meeting his gaze straight on. "You already know it is. Same as I know Vin Collins sent the two of you to deliver a message to me. Ganzer was the carrot. You two must be the stick. Which means your job is to make it clear that if I don't do what Vin wants, I'm going to regret it. Right?"

The bald one standing to one side of her narrowed his eyes. "How'd you know that?"

"Because Vin isn't one for subtlety or finesse. I can save us all a lot of time and effort here. I'm not scared of Vin or the two of you, so tell your boss that I'm not going to agree to meet with him. That ship left orbit a long time ago, and it's not coming back."

"He said you'd say something like that," the one in front of her said.

"Then he's already prepared to be disappointed. Perfect. That makes this so much easier, doesn't it? You two can fly back and tell him he was right for once."

The one in front of her flicked a glance to his partner, who had moved out of her line of sight and was now somewhere behind her. "I don't think so. Vin would be pissed. His orders were pretty clear. He wants you to meet with him, and he wants it to happen soon."

The one behind her spoke next. "We're here to make sure you make the meeting, so this is how things are going to go. You're going to invite me on board, and we're going to take a little trip together."

Zura didn't bother turning around. If she did, she had a hunch the one she was currently facing would grab her and the fight would be on that much sooner. "Like hell we are. I'm not going anywhere with either of you. If Vin thinks that sending a couple of goons is going to make me change my mind about meeting with him, then he's even more of a *fraxxing* idiot than he used to be," she said, stalling for time as she ran through her options.

Not that she had many options to choose from. Screaming for help and hoping for a random white knight to rush in and rescue her wasn't really in her nature, which left her with two choices. Run for it, or fight.

The big guy took a step toward her, and she reached for the neural disruptor she kept hidden in a wrist sheath. Running would only postpone this confrontation. She had to stand her ground here and now.

That was when a new voice joined the conversation. "If either of you assholes lay a hand on her, I'll break every bone in your body—in alphabetical order."

Zura knew that voice. Apparently her white knight had arrived, and she hadn't even needed to scream.

She risked a quick glance backward and spotted Luke standing a few feet behind her. His expression was murderous as he glared at the bald man he had by the throat while he held him suspended half a foot off the deck.

"Gentlemen, meet my friend, Luke. Did Vin's orders mention what to do if you pissed off a cyborg during our little conversation?" she asked.

"A *fraxxing* cyborg?" the one in front of her asked, his face rapidly turning a remarkable shade of puce as he stared over her head to where Luke was standing. "We weren't going to hurt her. We were talking. That's all."

"I'm pretty sure Zura's done with this conversation. You done, gorgeous?"

"I've got nothing else to say to these two. They can go back to their boss and tell him my answer is no," she said, drawing the disruptor and setting it to its highest power level.

Luke tossed the one he held against the far wall of the corridor, and Zura felt a surge of satisfaction as the man hit it with a meaty thud, still gasping for air.

"Five minutes. Be gone in five minutes, or the only message your boss is going to get from you will be spelled out with your body parts."

Luke was hanging onto his control by a thread. He wanted to kill these two for even coming close to Zura. The only thing that stopped him was the fact that they hadn't actually done anything illegal, yet. This far from civilization, the only laws were the ones corporation security forces chose to enforce, but outright assault was still frowned on. They really couldn't afford the fines that would come if Corp-Sec decided to enforce the rules this time.

The two men bolted like a pair of frightened rabbits. The second they were out of sight, Luke activated his comm device and made a call to Kit. He could have contacted him via their internal link, but he wanted Zura to hear what was said. "Zura had more visitors. She's okay, but if you can swing it, I'd like to take a look at the footage from the docking bay by Zura's ship. Maybe our friends can help us identify the two idiots I just sent packing."

"What the *fraxx* is going on? You need me there?" Kit demanded.

"I don't know what's happening, yet. Zura's going to explain things to me in a second. We're good for now. Talk to you soon."

"I'll make the call. Don't let her out of your sight until you know what's happening," Kit said and disconnected their call.

"So, uh. Thanks for the assist," Zura said.

"You're welcome. Care to explain why it was needed?" he asked.

"Not really. Care to explain why you're down here when your shift doesn't end for hours?" she asked.

"I would have thought that was obvious. I was making sure you got back to the *Sun Sprite* okay. After your earlier visitor, Kit and I thought someone should keep an eye on you."

She folded her arms across her chest and sighed. "I can take care of myself."

He arched a brow at her. "I know you can. That doesn't mean I'm going to stop looking out for you.

You could have gotten hurt. I'm not leaving you alone again until I know the reason why."

"What's gotten into you and Kit tonight? I'll be fine. I promise. I can handle Vin Collins and his goons. That's his name, by the way. He's the reason for my earlier visitor and the two you just sent packing. Vin and I used to date. I left, and he hasn't accepted the fact that I am never going back to him. Vin always had a problem understanding that I have a mind of my own and that he was not in charge of my life. Sort of like a certain cyborg who followed me back to my ship tonight. Do you do that often?"

"What's gotten into us? In a word, you. Do I follow you home often? Nope, this was the first time. I would have offered to walk you back, but I know you would've said it wasn't necessary, and you would have been wrong." He didn't bother telling her that he had every intention of walking her everywhere she needed to go from now on. He would fight that battle another time.

"While I appreciate your concern, it wasn't necessary. You don't need to watch out for me, Luke. I'm used to taking care of myself."

"In case you haven't figured it out yet, you matter to us, Zura. Of course we're going to watch out for you." He walked up to her and set a finger under her chin, tipping her head back so he could look into her silver eyes.

"What are you doing?" she asked softly.

"Losing my mind, apparently." He leaned down and brushed his mouth across hers once before claiming her lips in a heated kiss. He knew the timing was terrible, and he didn't care. Seeing her stand up to those two men tonight had flipped a switch inside him. She might not understand that she was his to protect, but he knew better. He had waited long enough for Kit to get with the program. It was time to make their intentions clear.

Zura's heart was thundering in her ears as Luke kissed her for the first time. She hadn't expected this, but within seconds of their mouths meeting, she knew it was what she wanted. He turned her slightly and walked her backward a few steps so that she was up against the door to her ship. Caught between the cold metal of the door and his powerful body, all Zura could do was hold on for dear life as he kissed her again and again.

His kisses were hot, hard, and full of fire. His tongue swiped over her lower lip, and when she opened her mouth to him, he groaned and kissed her harder. She barely noticed when he took hold of her arm and lifted it so that her palm passed over the access panel. It wasn't until the door slid open that she realized what he had done.

With nothing to support her, she started to fall backward, only to find herself caught fast in his arms. He carried her the rest of the way onto the ship, setting her back on her feet once they were safely inside.

"Pack a bag," he told her.

"What? Why?"

"You don't actually think I'm going to leave you here alone after what happened, do you? You're staying with us until we figure this out."

"Oh no. I just moved back onto the *Sun Sprite*," she argued, doing her best to ignore how sexy he was at that moment.

"Pack. A. Bag."

"No. I don't need to pack because I'm not going anywhere. We both know I can't do my job if I'm hiding from Vin at the Nova. Not to mention the fact that neither you nor Kit are in a position to tell me what to do."

He gave her a lopsided grin that made her heart beat faster. "How about you consider it a strongly worded request instead? I'm not going to sleep unless I know you're safe."

She laughed at that. "Safe isn't a word that really applies to my life. You know that."

He sighed in frustration and ran a hand through his hair. "I do, but that doesn't mean I like it. You weren't even supposed to be back from your run until tomorrow morning, so how did Ganzer know where to find you? And those two goons were here, waiting for you despite the fact you only turned down the Jeskyran a short time ago. Whatever this Vin guy is after, he's serious about it. I think you should be, too."

Zura paused to consider what Luke said and conceded that he had a good point. Vin wasn't playing around. She still wasn't sure why he was so determined to get her back in his life, but it would be foolish to turn her back on an offer of help. There was no point in letting her pride get in the way. She made do on her own because she had to most of the time. This time, she had friends willing to step up.

She blew out a breath and nodded. "Okay then. I'll stay at the Nova tonight. I can make some calls and find out what the hell Vin's up to, and by tomorrow, I should start getting some answers. This is only temporary, though. I have contracts to work and a living to make."

"Thank you," Luke said and brushed a quick kiss across her cheek.

"No. Thank you. I appreciate you looking out for me, even if I didn't ask for it." She grabbed the front of his shirt and pulled him back down to her level so she could kiss him properly. If she was going to be reckless and give into temptation instead of taking the safe path, then dammit, she was going in full throttle. When the inevitable crash and burn came, it wouldn't matter what speed she was going, it was going to hurt no matter what.

CHAPTER THREE

Kit was up early despite the fact he had only managed to get a few hours of sleep. The club had stayed packed until closing time. Normally that would be a reason to celebrate, but instead, he had resented the fact it kept him away from Zura. For the first time in months, he wasn't interested in losing himself in work. He wanted to talk to her and find out what the *fraxx* was going on and how they could help.

Instead, Cyn had escorted Zura to her room and gotten her settled. Last time, Zura had stayed in one of the handful of rooms they rented out to customers. This time, they'd given her space in the employee quarters. There weren't many amenities, but it was comfortable and far safer. That part of the club could only be accessed by keycard, and the only ones who had them were staff members Kit knew he could trust.

His thoughts were racing, and the walls of his quarters were closing in on him by the time he finished his coffee. Today, he just couldn't face another breakfast of rehydrated eggs and synthetic bacon, so instead of getting something from the food dispenser and eating in his rooms, he headed to the kitchen to make himself real food. Cooking was something he enjoyed, even if he didn't get to do it often.

At this time of day, he expected the kitchen to be empty, but when he walked in, the lights were on, and he could hear someone humming to themselves from somewhere behind the pantry doors.

"Hello," he called out, wondering which of the kitchen staff was getting an early start. A quick glance told him that the grills were still powered down, the appliances were all still gleaming from their end-of-shift cleaning, and there wasn't so much as a crumb on the countertops. Whoever was here, they hadn't started prepping yet.

Zura popped into view and gave him a shy smile. She was holding a loaf of bread in one hand and a jar of peanut butter in the other. "Hey there. I woke up starving. I figured no one would mind if I made myself a sandwich."

"You're welcome to whatever you need, for as long as you want," he said.

"It's only temporary, Kit. A day or two at most. I have a run scheduled in a couple of days, and there's no way in hell I'm reneging on a contract because of Vin."

"Why don't you tell me about him while I cook us something to eat? I can promise it will be a lot tastier than a peanut butter sandwich."

"You cook?" she asked, surprised.

"I do. It's something I learned after I was released from service. For years, I had to eat what I was given, usually food tabs with about as much flavor as a floor tile. I wanted to be able to make myself whatever I wanted, whenever I wanted to eat it."

"That makes sense. Did Luke learn, too?"

"He gave it a shot, but it's not his most impressive skill. In fact, he's actually banned from using the kitchen unless he's being supervised."

"If you're cooking, then I'm happy to abandon my plans for sandwiches. In fact, I'll make you a deal. You tell me why your brother isn't allowed to cook, and I'll tell you about the lapse in judgment that was my time with Vin Collins."

"Done." Kit felt a flush of jealousy at the thought of her being with anyone else. Logically he knew that she'd been with this Vin guy before the three of them even met, but he still didn't like the idea of anyone else touching her. His head still wasn't sure this was the right thing for all of them, but his heart seemed to be on another trajectory already. One headed straight for her.

"Then I'll put this stuff back for the next time I'm in need of a snack."

"Did you sleep well?" he asked, crossing the kitchen to join her at the pantry.

"I did. I would have slept just fine on the *Sun Sprite*, though."

"You were safer here with us," he said.

"If I didn't think that, I wouldn't be here."

"I'm glad you're here." Before he knew what he was doing, he had her soft cheek cupped in his hand. The moment he touched her, he knew it wasn't going to be enough.

One touch and he was on fire. Without a word, he leaned down to slant a kiss across her full lips.

She fisted the fabric of his shirt in her hands, using the leverage to pull herself up onto her toes as she kissed him back. Lust slammed into him and sent his senses reeling. He was hard within seconds. His heart was thundering in his chest as he wrapped his free arm around Zura's waist and tugged her in tight to his body. She fit against him perfectly, her soft body welcoming and lush in his arms.

Being in Kit's arms wasn't what Zura had planned when she left her room and gone to the kitchen this morning, but she wasn't going to complain about the unexpected direction her day had taken. As wake-ups went, this was a hell of a lot better than a cup of coffee. Kit's kisses were better than even her imagination had conjured. He was demanding and possessive, and his touch was confident but tender. His chest was warm beneath her fingers, and every breath she took carried his subtle, spicy scent into her lungs. Even after he lifted his mouth from hers, she didn't let go of him. She liked the way it felt to be nestled in his arms.

"If you don't let go of me, I'm going to have trouble making us something to eat," Kit said with amusement. He moved his hand from her cheek to drop his hand down and tap her fingers.

"I'm enjoying the moment. You and your brother both have a problem with your timing, you know that, right? You could have kissed me weeks ago."

He went still for a moment. "Weeks, huh? Why didn't you say anything?"

"I...I guess I didn't think you'd be interested. I mean, the two of you are sexy as hell, successful, and every time I saw you, you were both surrounded by beautiful women."

"What other women? The only one I've noticed is you. In case you haven't guessed by now, we're very interested. I just needed to deal with some baggage first."

"Andrea?" She asked, barely daring to utter the other woman's name.

"Andrea," he confirmed. "She had me convinced that no woman would ever want to be in a real relationship with something like us."

She pulled her head back far enough she could look up at him. "You're not a thing. None of you are things. So, you've got some machine parts and some nifty software implanted that lets you do things average people can't. I'm *blue*, Kit. I'm the last person in the cosmos who is going to judge someone on who, or what, they are."

He groaned her name and held her tightly. "I think you're the sexiest woman I've ever met. Not to mention, blue is my favorite color."

She laughed and tweaked his dark blue shirt between her fingers. "I would never have guessed."

The décor of the Nova was all done in shades of blue. From the color of the tables, to the lighting, to the staff uniforms, it was all either blue or gleaming chrome. If the brothers didn't like blue, they would have to be masochistic to go with that color scheme.

He kissed her again, wrapping her hair around his fingers as his tongue swept across the crease of her lips. When he finally lifted his head, his eyes were glittering with barely checked desire.

"Definitely my favorite color," he murmured.

"I think cyborg might be my new favorite everything." She didn't realize she had spoken out loud until it was too late. "*Fraxx,* forget I said that. Your kiss short-circuited my filter for a second."

"Forget it? Not a chance." He tapped his temple with one finger. "Cyborg advantage, we have total recall of all events, forever."

"Great," she muttered as a blush stole over her cheeks. She hated it when she blushed. Instead of turning pink or red like the humans she grew up around, she turned a deeper shade of blue, and the stripes on her face and neck darkened almost to black.

"Oh damn, that's sexy," he tugged on her hair until she lifted her head so he could see her face more clearly. "Is that what happens when you blush? If it is, I'm going to be trying to make you blush all the time, little one."

"It's weird, not sexy."

"There's nothing weird about you, Zura. You just finished telling me that I'm not a thing, I'm a man. Well, you're a beautiful woman. It doesn't matter to me if you're human, or Pheran, or Torski for that matter. You're the woman I want to spend time with."

She blew out a slow breath. "This is really happening? I mean, us. This. Whatever this is."

His lips quirked up into a slow, sensual grin. "Apparently, yes. This is happening. You, me, and Luke."

"And it's the three of us, together? This trio thing is new to me. I feel a little guilty about kissing you both."

"Never feel guilty for sharing your affections with Luke. Now, if you share them with anyone else, we'll have a problem. We only share with each other." Kit hugged her before finally releasing her from the confines of his arms.

"I don't share, either. That's one of the many reasons I'm no longer with Vin." Zura let go of Kit's shirt and took a step back so she could look up into his handsome face. The brothers were both tall enough she was going to wind up with a permanent crick in her neck.

"Do you think he wants you back because he realized he was a fool to let you go in the first place? Is it you he wants, or is he after something else?" Kit asked as he started selecting ingredients from the pantry.

"I have no *fraxxing* clue what that vermin wants with me, to be honest. He should know I'm never going back to him or that life." She hopped up onto an empty expanse of counter and got comfortable. "I'll explain while you cook. What are you making us?"

"Strawberry pancakes. We got in a shipment of frozen berries not long ago, and I had the cooks set some aside for me. That sound good to you?" he asked.

"It sounds amazing. I've never had a guy offer to cook for me before."

"I don't get a chance to do this very often. Usually, I use the food dispenser in my room."

"No room for a real kitchen in your quarters?" she asked. She knew she was supposed to be talking about Vin, but she really didn't want to. She had done all she could to leave the mistakes of her past behind her.

"Not really. Our quarters aren't much bigger than the one you're staying in. It's still a huge improvement over the way we lived when we were soldiers, though."

"I bet. At least here you have your own space, even if it isn't much. My room here is simpler than the last one, but I have to admit even it has more amenities than the *Sun Sprite*."

Kit chuckled. "I've been on enough space vessels to know that they're never designed for comfort."

"The *Sun Sprite*'s no exception. I could spend some scrip and make it nicer, but I'd rather invest in keeping her running in peak condition. You're welcome to come onboard and visit anytime you like, you know. There's not much to see, but it's my home."

"I'd enjoy seeing your ship," he said, moving around the kitchen as he started preparing their meal. "How long have you lived on board?"

"All my life," she answered with a casual shrug.

Kit turned to stare at her. "All your—you were born on board?"

"I was born on a station in the Castor system, but I wasn't there long. My Pheran mother was a waitress in a club not that different from this one. I probably would have grown up there, but my mother died when I was born. Her family sent a message to my father, letting him know what happened. Dad came to get me as soon as he could. I grew up on the *Sun Sprite*, traveling from port to port with him."

"He took you with him? Who took care of you when he was working?" Kit asked, his expression somewhere between curiosity and dismay. He might have had no childhood at all, but at least he hadn't been dragged around the galaxy while he was still an impressionable child.

"Where he went, I went. At least until I was old enough to be left on board by myself. To put it mildly, I had a very colorful and varied upbringing. I know the inside of every dive bar, pleasure house, and gambling den between here and the far end of the galaxy."

"How many worlds have you been to?"

"I've lost count. Some of them don't really count since I never left the port area. Often, I never got closer than orbit. It was just the two of us for a long time, going where the cash and contracts led us."

"So that was your life? Flying around the galaxy with your father?"

She nodded. "Pretty much. Later on, my brother joined us, but his mother never let him stay for long."

"You have a brother? You've never mentioned him."

"Half-brother, actually. Royan. Dad never told me about him, and I had no idea he even existed until we were both twelve or so. That was when his mother finally told him who his father was and where to find him."

"Your father never told you that you had a brother?" Kit asked incredulously.

"He wasn't allowed to see Royan. Once she found out about me, Royan's mother didn't want my dad near her or her son. I don't think he knew how to tell me about it, so he didn't."

"Then suddenly you're twelve and discover you have a sibling? How'd that go? Is he half-Pheran, too?"

"It was weird at first, but nothing about my childhood was ever really normal. Royan was a much nicer surprise than some others I can recall. My brother is full human. I'm the only blue one in the family."

Kit wandered back to her and held up a gooey, freshly thawed strawberry between his fingers. "Snack?"

She held out her hand, and he shook his head. "No sense in both of us getting messy. Open your mouth, little one. I'll feed it to you."

She felt a little foolish but opened her mouth. Kit fed her the fruit gently, and she couldn't resist sucking on his fingers as he did it. His eyes blazed with heat, and she thought she heard a hint of groan roll up from his chest.

"Do that again, and I'll feed you every damned berry we've got right here and now. Screw the pancakes."

She pretended to pout. "You said you'd make me pancakes. I have to say that I am really enjoying watching you cook. The view is pretty spectacular."

"The view, huh?" Kit asked. He was enjoying their conversation, but something told him that Zura was keeping the topic light on purpose. Whatever happened between her and Vin, she wasn't in a hurry to talk about it.

"Oh, yeah. You have to know you look good dressed like that. Snug pants and those form-fitting shirts. Why do you think I came here so often in the beginning, before I knew you? The food isn't *that* good. I come for the view, and I'm not the only one who does." She leered and waggled her brows at him and then burst out laughing.

"Please don't tell Luke that. His ego doesn't need the boost."

"No, it really doesn't," she agreed once she stopped laughing.

"Tell me about Vin, little one. I need to know who we're dealing with."

Zura sighed. "I should start by telling you that my dad wasn't the most law abiding of men. He did what was necessary to keep me fed and clothed, and the *Sun Sprite* flying. Sometimes that meant black market runs and even outright smuggling. To find that kind of work you needed contacts, and that led to making friends with people of…let's say they were of dubious character. One of them was a guy named Vin Collins. He was only a few years older than I was, and he talked a good game. Vin ran with a rough crowd, but he managed to send a fair bit of business Dad's way. I'm still not sure how it happened, but somewhere along the way, Vin and I sort of fell into a relationship."

"Your father let you go out with someone he knew was a criminal?" Kit asked, trying, and failing, to keep the judgment out of his voice.

"I'm more than old enough to be with whoever the hell I want to, and there weren't a whole lot of options at the time. We lived a rough life, and I kept even rougher company. It was the only way I knew how to be.

"It wasn't long after we got together that my dad died. At first, Vin was there for me, helping me deal with the aftermath. I was in a daze and barely able to remember to eat and sleep, never mind fulfill Dad's contractual obligations and deal with his debts. It took me a while to start noticing things were off. I thought Vin was taking care of me. Turns out, he was only looking out for himself. The bastard."

"What was he doing? And what happened to your father? I knew you lost him, but you've never mentioned how it happened."

"There's not much to tell, really. It happened less than a year ago. He made the mistake of accusing the wrong man of cheating him at cards, and it got him killed. They caught the guy who did it a few days later. He wasn't smart enough to even get rid of the murder weapon. It was an open and shut case."

"I'm sorry, Zura. That must have been terrible to deal with. Luke and I have lost a lot of friends over the years, but we always had each other to lean on. You were alone." He walked away from the stove and straight to where she was sitting, gathering her into his arms and tucking her head beneath his chin.

She snuggled into him with a gentle sigh that made him want to keep her sheltered like this for the rest of her life.

"It was the worst time of my life. Royan offered to help, but I knew he wanted to be on his own, so I didn't tell him how bad things really were. If I hadn't been so messed up, I would have noticed what Vin was doing sooner. Contracts started showing up with his name on them instead of mine. He told me it was a clerical error, and he would get it cleared up. He didn't. I went to pay for some parts and discovered there wasn't enough money in the account to cover the purchase even though there should have been. I started checking into things and discovered Vin had arranged for payments to go to him, not to me.

"He had all sorts of excuses, but eventually, I stopped believing anything he said. He kept asking me if my dad had an insurance policy. He started getting obsessed over it. Like I was secretly hiding a fortune somewhere, and the whole living hand-to-mouth thing was a ruse. I think he thought he could get more money out of me, which was a laugh. All I inherited from my dad was the *Sun Sprite*, his contracts, and a whole lot of debt."

"How did it end?"

"Badly. He came home one night, drunk out of his head and angry. He kept raving on about my inheritance. He wasn't making any sense, and I told him so. Things got heated, and well, he hurt me. Badly. I don't remember much. The reports say I stunned him and dragged myself off the ship. I woke up in a medical center, and once they let me go, I left for good. Royan flew with me for a while, but eventually he went his own way, and I wound up out on the Drift."

"That son of a bitch. If Vin ever comes near you again, I'll do more than stun his sorry ass. All that, and now he sends guys to try and get you to meet with him? It doesn't make any sense."

She shrugged. "He was never one for subtlety. His skill set is more along the lines of intimidation and chest thumping until he gets his way. I'm not going back, though. I left all that behind and started over again. No more smuggling. No illegal cargo. No Vin."

"He's definitely not going for subtle. Then again, if Luke hadn't followed you last night, this might have all gone unnoticed by anyone but you. Vin miscalculated, though. You're not alone. You've got us in your corner."

"I do." She lifted her head and kissed the corner of his mouth.

"You're cuddling on a countertop? I'm pretty sure that's some kind of health violation. And while I hate to break up this touching moment, you're burning my breakfast," Luke said as he wandered into the kitchen.

"The pancakes! *Veth*!" Kit cursed and kissed Zura one last time before dashing back across the kitchen to rescue breakfast.

"Now that I've got him out of the way—good morning, gorgeous." Luke had a hunch he would find his brother cooking, but he hadn't expected to find Zura there. Since she was, he was more than happy to claim his brother's place. He kissed her gently and wrapped an arm around her shoulders, holding her close.

"Good morning to you, too. That was very smooth, by the way," she said and kissed him back

He winked at her, pleased to see her smiling. "I thought so, too."

"What did I tell you about complimenting him, Zura?" Kit asked.

"I hope he told you to do it often and with great enthusiasm," Luke said as he stole another kiss.

"Not even close," she replied.

"If you've been badmouthing me, then you and I are going to be having words later."

Kit finished rescuing the pancakes and turned around, a spatula still in his hand. "I said nothing that wasn't true. And who said anything about me cooking your breakfast? These are for Zura and I. You want food, Luke, you can make it yourself."

"I thought you said he was banned from cooking?" Zura asked with a snicker.

"You told her about that? So, that's how it's going to be, huh? In that case, I've got some great pictures of Kit after he lost a bet to Cyn. He looks totally adorable with bows in his hair and this fantastic shade of lipstick she picked out for him. Hang on, I'll pull them up."

"Don't you *fraxxing* dare. You swore to me you deleted those things years ago," Kit grumbled.

"I lied. There's no way I'm giving up my best blackmail material."

"Asshole," Kit swore at him.

"Love you too. If you send some of those pancakes this way, I might be persuaded not to show Zura how good you look in pink."

"'Fine, I'll make you breakfast. Zura, don't you believe him; I have never worn anything pink."

"He's right. My mistake. I'm pretty sure the lipstick was more of a mauve. Shall I pull up the photos and confirm?"

Zura was laughing so hard her cheeks were flushed, and there were tears rolling down her cheeks. "This is how you two treat each other when I'm not around?"

"Yeah. We can only abuse each other when we're off-duty. The rest of the time, we need to be a united front. You think you can cope with that?" Luke asked. While he talked, he coiled an indigo colored lock of her hair around his finger. He had always been fascinated by her multi-hued hair, and now he was finally free to play with it, and any other part of her she wanted him to.

"Honestly? I like it. My brother and I never really knew each other well enough to tease each other like that. If he had stuck around, maybe we would have gotten there eventually."

"Wait, brother? What brother?" Luke asked. He was damned sure he hadn't heard about Zura having any siblings.

"See what you miss when you sleep in? She's got a younger brother named Royan. I meant to ask, how much younger? Did he grow up on a station, too?' Kit said.

"Royan's three months younger than I am, and no, he wasn't a station kid. He was born on Earth, a true Terran. His mom didn't want him to have anything to do with Dad. She hated him, actually. Because of me."

"You were born three months apart?" Luke sputtered. "Gee, I wonder why she didn't like him."

Zura nodded. "Exactly. My dad had some good qualities, but an appreciation for the concept of monogamy wasn't one of them. He showed up a few days after Royan's birth with me in his arms, and Roy's mother threatened to shoot him where he stood. At least that's the story I always heard."

Luke blinked. "Interesting family you have."

"Believe me, I know."

"So, where is your brother now? Should we expect a visit at some point when he finds out you're with us and decides to check out his sister's new boyfriends?" Kit asked.

"Last time we talked, he was crewing on a long haul freighter for one of the corporations. I don't expect him to visit. Like I said, we're not that close. We spent too many years apart growing up. We keep in contact, but we have very separate lives. Besides, I'm a grown woman. He doesn't get a say in my love life one way or another."

Luke shook his head. "You're wrong. Brothers do get a say. It can be blatantly ignored, but they get a say."

"I'd like to see you try and tell Cyn who she can and cannot date. You could book a cage match and sell tickets," she replied then added, "and who said I was with the two of you? Two kisses and an offer of a dinner date that we haven't actually had yet hardly constitutes being with someone." She wasn't sure she believed that, but it was fun to tease them. It was too soon to know what this was, or how it was going to go. With her luck, she wouldn't have long before this ride was over and their friendship burned up on re-entry.

"You're with us," both men spoke at once.

Zura couldn't help it, she burst out laughing. "Did you two rehearse that?"

"We didn't need to. There was only one answer to your question. We didn't kiss you on a whim, little one. We knew what we were doing." Kit turned around and came over to join them with two plates full of pancakes in his hands. They were smothered in strawberries and whipped cream, and Zura's stomach rumbled at the sight.

Kit handed one of the dishes to his brother and kept one for himself. "Hey, where's mine?" she asked nodding to the plates.

"Right here," Luke said, offering her the first bite of his breakfast.

"First, Kit, now you. I can feed myself, you know," Zura protested.

"We know. But this is more fun," Luke said as he wiggled the tempting morsel in front of her.

"Not to mention, fewer dishes this way," Kit pointed out as he took a bite of his pancake.

"And there goes my appetite," Cyn groaned as she walked into the kitchen and spotted the three of them.

"Morning, Cyn," Zura said, pulling back from Luke's offering to look at their sister. Cyn Armas was everything Zura had dreamed of being when she was a girl. She had long legs, a perfect body, and the face of an angel. She wore her hair in a short pixie cut that somehow only enhanced her features, and not even the jagged scar that ran along the right side of her jaw detracted from her beauty. On top of that, Cynder was one of the brightest, most capable women Zura had ever met, and she had confidence to spare.

"Good morning. Don't mind me, I'm just here for coffee. I didn't mean to interrupt you adorable lovebirds." Cyn clasped a hand over her heart, fluttered her dark lashes, and smirked at the three of them.

"Something wrong with the coffee in your room, Cyn?" Kit asked.

"Yeah, there isn't any. I forgot to restock with all the chaos last night. You can go back to your breakfast seduction scene in a few minutes. Oh, and Kit, I'm glad to see you're in such a good mood this morning. It's a big improvement over last night." She waited for a half a beat before adding. "I *fraxxing* told you so. Next time, save us all some time and don't argue with me."

Luke chuckled. "You're going to pay for that one, Cyn."

"I know, but it'll be worth it." She grinned as she filled her coffee mug.

"Zura, one word of advice before I go. Don't let Luke cook you anything. I like you, little blue, and I'd hate to lose you to food poisoning." Cyn gave them a jaunty wave, turned on her booted heel, and headed back through the door she had entered by.

"Don't listen to her. I've never poisoned anyone," Luke said.

Kit lifted a forkful of syrupy pancake to her lips. "He's right. No one has ever eaten anything he's tried to cook. Too burnt to even identify."

"I might not be able to cook, but I was gifted with many other talents, thank you," Luke retorted.

She took Kit's offering and moaned in pleasure at the flavor exploding on her tongue. When it was gone, she dipped her finger into Luke's whipped cream and sucked it off her fingertip before answering. "I can't cook that well either. I'm a better mechanic than I am a cook."

Both men watched her, riveted as she licked the cream from her finger.

"Damn. That was…" Kit said.

"Totally," Luke agreed.

Zura scooped a bit of whipped cream and strawberry juice from both their plates onto her index fingers and held out a hand to each of them. "Your turn. If you get to feed me, I get to feed you, too."

Kit moved a split-second faster than Luke, but a second later both had drawn her fingers into their mouths. Sparks of arousal danced along her skin, and heat pooled between her thighs at the sensation. *Re'veth.* If this was how it felt to be with two men, then she was in deep trouble. The kind of trouble a girl could happily drown in.

CHAPTER FOUR

Zura sat at her favorite table at the Nova and sorted through the messages she had received. She had contacted everyone she trusted, looking for information on Vin. Her inquiries into his recent activities weren't producing much in the way of useful information. All she knew for sure was that he had somehow managed to become a man to be reckoned with in the months since she had left. She couldn't understand how that had happened, given that the Vin Collins she knew wasn't blessed with an overabundance of brainpower or charisma.

"If Vin's a man of influence and power now, then standards among the criminal element have plummeted since I left," she muttered to herself as she scanned a message from yet another contact. There was nothing in it that she didn't already know. No one had any idea why, but Vin hadn't lost interest in her during the time she had been gone.

She had also figured out how Vin had tracked her to the far edge of civilized space. It was all because of the vaccine she had delivered during the cosmic storm. At the time, it had never occurred to her that what she'd done would be of interest to anyone beyond the Drift. It probably wouldn't have been more than a footnote in local history, except that the corporations had decided to pay for the repairs to her ship and given her a nice chunk of bonus pay. It was great publicity for them, and she had been too sick at the time to do more than say thank you to the corporate reps who had shown up to give her the news.

Her dad always said that no good deed went unpunished. This time, he had been right.

There wasn't any point in regrets, though. What was done, was done, and the lives of the people she had been able to help save were far more important than the annoyance of having Vin back in her life. She would deal with him and get back to the life she was forging for herself out here.

She had a supply run to prep for soon. It was a short haul that wouldn't take more than a few days each way, on a route she could fly with her eyes closed. It was easy work, which was her favorite kind, but she still needed time to prepare and go over the ship. Reality was waiting for her, and she had to get back to it if she wanted to have scrip to pay for the little things in life, like food and docking fees for the *Sun Sprite*.

She glanced around the bar as she pondered everything waiting for her outside the Nova's walls. The evening rush hadn't started yet, which meant the bar was as close to quiet as it got during business hours. Quiet was a relative thing, though. Even now, there was music thrumming from more than a dozen speakers, the sound blending with the murmur of voices from the few patrons enjoying an early start to the night's revelry.

The games tables were doing a steady business already, parting miners and crewman from their hard earned scrip.

She had claimed her favorite table again, and the view out her window was one she could enjoy for hours. The *Sun Sprite* was docked out there, hanging in space against a backdrop of stars. It reminded her of being in the cockpit of her ship, staring out into the cosmos as she flew from place to place.

She considered ordering something to snack on, but she didn't want to ruin her appetite for dinner. Luke had sent her a message reiterating his invitation for her to dine with the two of them tonight. When she had agreed, he had let her know they were in a meeting and would come find her once they were done.

While she waited, it occurred to her that she was going on her first real date with them, and she didn't have anything decent to wear. She knew it wasn't logical. They had known each other for months, but tonight was special, and she wanted to mark the occasion by dressing for it. Unfortunately, most of her clothes were hanging in her closet on her ship, and they had made her promise that she wouldn't leave the club unescorted. After what had happened last night, she understood their concern, so she grudgingly agreed.

She caught sight of one of the club's security guards walking between the tables and in a flash of inspiration, flagged him down.

"Hey, Zura. I heard a rumor you were staying with us again. Welcome back," Owen greeted her.

"Hi, Owen. The rumors are true. It's only temporary, though. Do you have a minute? I've got a favor to ask." She gestured to one of the empty chairs, silently inviting him to join her.

"I heard you were attacked last night," he said as he claimed the closest chair.

"Attacked is a pretty strong word for what happened. Someone I used to know is trying to convince me to meet with him, and I'm not interested. When I declined, he sent two of his goons to try and change my mind. Luke sent them packing."

The guard grinned. "Luke was with you? Does this mean the other rumor I heard today is true, too?"

She groaned. "Tell me you haven't already heard gossip about us. We only really got started last night!"

Owen chuckled. "I'm afraid so. I heard that Kit and Luke were seen cooking for a certain cargo pilot in the main kitchen today. This is a tight-knit little community, Zura. Happy news travels fast."

"I'd sort of hoped no one would notice for a while, but I guess that wasn't very realistic of me, was it? We're having our first real date tonight. Since they made me swear I wouldn't leave the club without an escort, I was wondering if maybe you might be free to walk over to the *Sun Sprite* so I can pick up something nice to wear. I didn't pack more than a quick overnight bag before coming here and dressing for dinner wasn't really on my mind at the time."

"I'm more than happy to do anything that will put a smile on Kit's face. C'mon, if we go now, we should be back before they even know you've been gone."

The moment she nodded, Owen rose and led the way to the front doors and past the security guard standing at the entrance. "I'm taking Zura to her ship for a few minutes. If Kit or Luke happen to come looking for her, tell them she's with me."

"Why do I feel like I'm breaking out of prison instead of merely going to get a change of clothes?" she muttered as she followed Owen out into the station.

"We take security seriously. You're not used to noticing it, is all. Now that you're with Luke and Kit, things will be different."

"We haven't even gone on a proper date yet. I'm not sure what our official status is at the moment," she said.

Owen slowed his pace and fell in beside her. "I wouldn't worry about qualifications or labels. We all know they like you, and clearly you feel the same way, or we wouldn't be on our way to pick up something for you to wear tonight. I meant what I said about Kit, too. I actually saw him smile today, and I'm betting that's because of you."

"Getting your heart stomped on is enough to make anyone grumpy for a while. From what little I've heard, though, she was a bitch. I may not be the one for them, but I won't treat them the way she did; they deserve better."

"Remind him of that, will you? Maybe he'll listen to you, because he's too damned stubborn to listen to the rest of us."

"He hasn't been listening to me so far. Neither of them are. They were the ones that insisted I stay at the club last night, and there was no talking them out of it."

Owen snorted. "That sounds like them."

"I guess it's sort of sweet that the guys are so protective, though. Annoying, but sweet," she admitted.

"I've never heard those two described as sweet before. They must really be trying to impress you."

"Or maybe I have a weakness for big, stubborn males," she said as they arrived at the door that accessed her ship.

"I would say that's a fair assessment. Otherwise, you'd probably be having dinner with someone else tonight. I'll stand guard out here while you grab what you need," Owen said.

"You really don't need to do that."

"Oh, yeah, I do. Being alone with you on a locked ship is not a good idea. Your *sweet* men might tear my head off when they find out."

Zura huffed. "If they give you any grief for playing bodyguard, tell them to take it up with me." She left Owen standing guard and headed into her ship. She knew what outfit she wanted to wear tonight; she just needed to remember where the hell she had put it. In her line of work, it wasn't often she needed to wear a dress or all the accessories that went with it. Fortunately, Luke and Kit weren't fancy clothes and proper manners kind of guys, which suited her just fine.

* * * *

"This has to be the most uncomfortable thing I've ever worn," Luke grumbled as he tugged at the knot of his tie. He had only had the damned thing on for half an hour, and already, he wanted to tear it off and go back to his regular clothes.

"I have a new respect for anyone who has to wear these things every day. I have no idea how they stand it. Why are these things still in fashion?" Kit asked, nodding in agreement.

They had spent the afternoon making plans and picking up everything they needed for their date with Zura. After breakfast, he and Kit talked, and both of them agreed that they wanted tonight to be special. They would slow things down and show Zura they were interested in more than a fling or a brief affair. They wanted to get to know her and see if the three of them had a future together. Their preparations had taken a few hours and the calling in of a few favors, but everything was finally ready.

Luke took one last look around the private party room they had transformed for the night and couldn't see anything left to do. "I guess it's time to pick up our date."

"Don't forget the flowers," Kit said.

"Got 'em." Luke lifted the vase of red and white roses off the table and cradled them in his arm. Why women were partial to flowers covered in sharp spines was a mystery to him, but the only florist on the entire station had insisted that roses were the way to go.

They arrived at Zura's room, and both of them took a moment to straighten their unfamiliar clothing before Luke activated the door chime to let Zura know they were there. The door slid back almost immediately, and all his carefully rehearsed words went out the airlock.

"You look incredible," he said, though incredible didn't do justice to the beauty standing in the doorway. Her hair fell around her shoulders like a silken cape. The little black dress she was wearing…holy *fraxx*. It barely fell to mid-thigh, and the V-neck plunged low enough to give him a tantalizing view of her cleavage. The only jewelry she wore was a simple gold ring strung on a gold chain.

"Stunning," Kit said.

"And you two look—wow. Are those roses?" Zura couldn't stop staring at her dates. They looked amazing. They were both wearing black slacks, crisp, white dress shirts buttoned up to the neck, and both of them had on elegantly patterned ties of different shades of blue. It was a far cry from their usual look, but damn if they didn't look amazing.

"For you." Luke offered her the red and white blooms.

"You brought me flowers? You didn't have to do that," she said, burying her face in the soft petals to inhale their fragrance. She had seen roses of course, but no one had ever bought them for her before. They had even placed them in a vase for her already.

"Chocolates, too," Kit announced. He produced a box from behind his back and presented it to her with a smile.

"Flowers and candy? You're going to spoil me. Thank you." She laughed and took the chocolates from him. "I hope you two are planning on helping me eat all these. If I eat the whole box, I'll have to diet for a week afterward."

Kit's eyes gleamed with desire as he drank in the sight of her. "We would be pleased to share them with you, little one, but there will be no more talk of diets," Kit said.

"Then I'll put the roses on my dresser and take the chocolates with us for dessert. Wait here one second, and I'll be right back," she said. She rushed to the bed, set down the roses and gave herself another quick look in the mirror. It was a good thing she had decided to grab something else to wear tonight, or she would've felt underdressed beside the two of them.

"I wasn't sure where we were going for dinner, and I didn't want to ask and spoil the surprise. Judging by your outfits, I take it we're going somewhere swanky?" she asked as she reappeared at the door.

"Somewhere private, actually," Luke said.

"With a door that locks so no one can walk in on us this time," Kit added.

"That sounds perfect." The idea of the three of them behind a locked door sent sparks of desire dancing down her spine.

They each offered her an arm and escorted her down to the main floor. Instead of heading to the club, though, they passed through an unfamiliar hallway and stopped at an unmarked door. Kit opened it with a wave of his hand, and Luke led her inside. Unsure what to expect, Zura looked around and let out a gasp of surprise.

"This must have taken you hours to set up." She looked around at what they had done. Soft music played in the background, a delicate tune that was light-years away from the pounding, bass-heavy tunes that normally played in the bar. There was an arrangement of red and white roses placed in the middle of a round table that was set for three. Lit candles were the only source of light, and there were more than a dozen of them in different sizes and shapes scattered throughout the room.

"Do you like it?" Kit asked.

"This is...you didn't have to go to all this trouble for me." Her throat tightened, and her cheeks heated as she turned back to look at her dates. "It's all gorgeous."

"No, Zura. You're the gorgeous one," Luke said before walking up and brushing a tender kiss to her lips. He took the box of chocolates from her and walked away to set them on a small table on the far side of the room.

Kit cleared his throat. "We wanted to do this. For you."

"Thank you I...wow. You two pulled out all the stops."

Kit took her hand and led her to the table. When she started to sit down, he stopped her with a touch, and then pulled out the chair for her.

"Would you like something to drink?" Luke asked her.

"I think I'm going to need a drink, yes, thank you." Zura couldn't believe all the trouble they had gone to. The roses, the decorated room, the clothes they were wearing. It made her feel special in a way she had never experienced before.

Luke went over to the bar and fixed them all drinks, though she couldn't see exactly what kind. When he turned around again, he was carrying three glasses of clear, bubbling liquid that looked familiar.

"Is that the same stuff we were drinking last night?" she asked.

"I promised you I would make a cocktail out of it and name it for you. I'm not finished tweaking the recipe, but I thought you'd like to be the first to try it." Luke set a glass down in front of her before claiming the seat to her left as Kit sat to her right.

"Before I try it, what's it called?" She eyed the cocktail with curiosity. It shifted colors every few seconds, from red to purple to blue and back again; the fog rising from the liquid overflowed the sides of the glass, making a pretty display.

"I haven't made a final decision yet, but I think it's going to be called '*Sun Sprite*'s Delight.' Rolls off the tongue, don't you think?"

She lifted the glass to get a better look. "You're naming it after my ship? That's awesome. Unless it tastes awful, in which case, I'm going to be insulted on her behalf."

"I would never do that to you or your ship. If I were going to make a lousy drink, I would've named it after Kit."

Kit glowered at his brother, then lifted his glass in toast. "To us. May tonight be the first of many we spend together."

"To us," Zura murmured, then took a sip of the cocktail. It was delicious, which didn't surprise her at all. "I'm not insulted. This is good."

"This isn't bad," Kit said.

"Of course it's good. I'm a brilliant bartender. Not to mention the fact I would never serve our love—lovely guest anything but the best."

Kit took another drink to hide his smile at his brother's slip. It should worry him how quickly they were thinking of Zura as their lover, but the truth was he was happy to know that his brother was as far gone as he was. He knew the moment he had fallen, too. It wasn't in the kitchen this morning or seeing her looking so beautiful when she opened her door tonight. It was when she looked at them with flushed cheeks and shining eyes and told them they shouldn't have gone to any trouble for her. He knew then that he would happily spend the rest of his life making her eyes light up that way.

A moment later, the door chimed, and he rose to his feet. He had left instructions for their meal to be left outside the door because he didn't want anyone else so much as stepping foot into this room tonight.

"You ordered delivery?" Zura joked.

"We decided to be selfish. We're not sharing you with anyone tonight," Kit said.

He waited until the corridor was silent once more before opening the door and retrieving the cart. After wheeling it in, Luke stood, and both of them made quick work of laying out the dishes they had decided on. It had taken some investigation of old orders she had placed and what the serving staff could remember, but they were confident they had managed to track down at least some of her favorite foods. Marinated olives and bite-sized peppers stuffed with melted cheese to start, followed by roasted chicken with stuffing and gravy.

Zura popped one of the olives into her mouth and moaned. "Where did you find these? They sure aren't the ones you serve in your martinis."

"You would be amazed what wonders I have tucked away in this place. When I come across something hard to find, I usually buy it and figure out what to do with it later," Luke said as he carved the chicken and served it to everyone, starting with Zura.

"Remind me to go snooping through the pantry later. I can't wait to see what else you've got stashed."

Luke gave her a sly grin. "If you want to go foraging for food, you're going to have to stick around. Only staff and family get free access to the back areas, you know that."

"What, no exceptions for your girlfriend?" she asked.

Kit blinked at her. "Did you just call yourself our girlfriend?"

"She did. I heard it," Luke said with no small amount of satisfaction.

Well, *fraxx*. She hadn't meant to say that. She started to blush, which made her feel even more awkward. "I didn't. I mean, I did, but I can take it back if you're not okay with it."

"I am very okay with you thinking of yourself that way, little one. As the head of security, I'm officially giving you permission to keep that key card once you go back to the *Sun Sprite*. Not that I want you to rush off. In fact, I'd like it if you postponed your next run. I don't like the idea of you going out there alone. What if Vin tries something again?"

"Then he'll find out that I made some extensive upgrades to my ship since last he was aboard. She's faster and far better armed."

Still feeling foolish over her slip, Zura lowered her gaze to her meal and took a mouthful of her dinner, trying to distract herself. When no one said anything, she looked up to find both of them looking at her with stormy expressions.

Finally, Kit sighed and rubbed the back of his neck. "If you want to go, we can't stop you. But dammit, Zura, you can't stop us from worrying about you, either."

"I guess I'm not used to having anyone to worry about me that way. Not since Dad died, anyway. I've been on my own for nearly a year, and risks are part of the job. If it helps, I have every intention of living to a ripe old age."

"Now you have someone who will worry. In fact, you have several someones. Why don't you have a crew, anyway? I always meant to ask," Luke asked.

"After I left Vin, and my brother left to do his own thing, I thought about hiring someone else, but there was no one I trusted enough. I was an infant when my dad came and got me from my Pheran relatives, and they've never reached out to me. Dad and Royan were the only family I knew. I decided I was better off alone and well-armed than flying with someone I couldn't depend on. Besides, no crew meant more money for me, and I needed every bit of scrip I could scrape together to keep flying, especially in the beginning. When dad died, he didn't have a will, so I got everything because I was the oldest. I didn't feel that was right, so I gave Royan half of what little there was. It left me with damned near nothing to pay off Dad's debts with, but it seemed to be the only fair thing to do."

"Fair, but not easy." Kit said.

"No, not easy," she said and shrugged. "Not everyone gets dealt a fair hand. We make do with what we're given and move on. I have to say, lately things have been going really well for me." *Like having dinner with the two of you.*

Luke surprised her by reaching out and taking her hand. "Things have definitely been looking up for us, too."

Kit took her other hand and squeezed it. "Which is why we're going to worry about you, little one. Not because we think you can't take care of yourself. We know you can. We protect what matters to us, and you matter. Very much."

"I'm glad I matter to you. I mean—you matter to me too. Both of you do." She held tight to their hands as she tried to calm the sudden storm of emotions churning inside her. Somewhere in the past few minutes, this had gone from a simple date to something more. She wasn't sure where this was going, but as she sat between them, holding both their hands, she knew that wherever tonight led, she wasn't going to let fear or doubt get in her way. Tonight, she was going to take a chance.

"I don't know about you, but right now, I think we should skip the rest of dinner and go straight to dessert," Luke said, his fingers caressing her palm.

She was about to agree when Kit cleared his throat and gave his brother an odd look.

"I'm not feeling very patient right now," Luke said out loud, despite the fact Kit hadn't said anything.

"Who said anything about being patient?" she asked.

Luke pointed to Kit. "He did. Only you didn't hear him because he was nagging me via our personal comm channel."

"You can talk to each other that way?"

"We can. We have internal comms with each other, with our batch siblings, and we used to be able to link up with any other cyborg in our battle group, if they were within range," Kit explained.

"That's incredible. You can't still do that?" she asked.

Luke shook his head. "We shut down the other channels when we left service. They're still there, just…quiet."

Zura understood the need for quiet. She liked the solitude of her life sometimes. Tonight though, tonight she didn't want to be alone. She had dreamed of being with them long enough already. It was time to seize the moment. "I know you think you need to be patient, Kit, but I'm with Luke. As amazing as this dinner has been, I think I'd rather skip to dessert. How does the three of us sharing the chocolates sound? Maybe while were all on that couch?" She nodded toward a large couch that took up most of the back wall.

"We don't want to rush you," Kit said.

"I'm not feeling rushed right now. Far from it. Besides, I think we're past worrying about rushing into anything. I've known you two for a while. I like you. A lot. I'm here because I want to be. If I were worried about being alone with you, I'd hardly have agreed to have dinner in a room with a locking door."

"But we were trying to show you—" Kit broke off without finishing his sentence.

"You don't need to show me you're good men. I already know that. You've done more for me already than any other man ever has. I've never been treated like this before. I feel spoiled, and I confess, I like it. That doesn't mean you need to change who you are or how you act to please me. I like you both no matter what you're wearing." She stood up, determined to make something clear. She walked up to Kit first and gently loosened his tie before unbuttoning his shirt, too.

"Better," she declared.

"In that case…" Luke muttered and snagged two fingers in his collar, tearing it open and sending several buttons flying.

She crooked a finger at them and walked backward until she was standing by the sofa. Taking a seat, she sat back, kicked off her shoes, and grinned at them despite the fact it felt like her heart was in her throat. "So, dessert now?"

"If dessert is what you want, then that's what you shall have," Luke said, already out of his chair and heading straight for her with desire gleaming in his dark eyes. He tore off his tie and dropped it on the floor along the way before undoing a few more buttons on his shirt.

Kit rose and went to the door, making a show of double checking the lock. "Last chance to leave, little one."

She shook her head. "I'm not going anywhere. I'm right where I want to be."

CHAPTER FIVE

Kit met Luke's eyes as he claimed a seat on the couch on the other side of Zura, and his brother's voice sounded inside his head. *"She's finally going to be ours."*

"Have I mentioned how stunning you look in that dress?" Luke asked out loud as he leaned in and kissed Zura.

"You did. I'm glad I went and got it this afternoon, or I would have been woefully underdressed for this evening's date."

Kit scowled. "You went and got it? From your ship? When? Who went with you?"

"Owen accompanied me. You two were busy, and I wanted to surprise you. Tonight was special, and I wanted to dress the part."

"You went with him? He's the biggest playboy on the payroll!" Kit turned and hauled her across his lap. "Don't go anywhere with him alone again."

"While Owen may be single, it would seem I'm not. Besides, he was a perfect gentleman. Unlike you, mister grabby hands. Why am I on your lap?"

"You're here because that seemed the best place for you after you told us that you were out and about with Owen." He kissed her hard, his hands busy stroking over every soft curvy inch of her he could reach.

"It's a good thing I think it's cute when you two get all grumpy and possessive," she whispered, her fingers busy undoing more of the buttons of his shirt.

"Just don't tell anyone you think of us that way," Luke said as he drew her legs across his lap.

"I may have told Owen I thought you two were sweet the way you were so protective of me," she confessed between kisses.

"How long did he laugh? And let me be clear: We're only sweet when it comes to you."

"I can live with that. As it happens, I only like grumpy, possessive men when it comes to the two of you, so I think we're even." Zura was finding it hard to think straight anymore. Both men had their hands on her, stroking and kissing her until she was half out of her mind.

"You say the nicest things," Luke crooned as he pulled out the box of chocolates and set it down on her legs. "Close your eyes. It's time we fed you dessert."

A shiver of anticipation coursed through her. This was turning out to be so much hotter than any fantasy she'd ever had about what it would be like to be with the brothers.

"I think we should make sure she doesn't peek. Luke, take your shirt off. Our girl here needs a blindfold."

"No, I don't," she protested. No sight meant no control, and that wasn't something she usually allowed.

Kit's lips brushed over hers. "Trust us, little one. You're going to enjoy this."

His words were a sensual promise, an invitation to something she didn't want to miss. Instead of arguing, she closed her eyes. It was time to follow her heart.

She could feel Luke moving, and then something soft was being placed over her face. It was still warm from his body heat and carried a trace of his scent in the fabric. As it was fastened in place, her heart began to beat a little faster. She knew she was soaking wet already, her thighs sticky with the proof of how aroused she was after only a few kisses and caresses.

"So how is this going to work?" she asked.

"You relax, and for once in your life, let someone take care of you the way you deserve," Kit whispered, nuzzling her ear so that his words were a soft buzz against her skin.

"We've got you, gorgeous. And I've got something for you...open your mouth for me."

She parted her lips and caught a whiff of chocolate a split second before a morsel landed on her tongue. Sweet. Sinful. It melted away in mere seconds, leaving her wanting more.

Again something brushed her lips, but this time it wasn't candy. Luke leaned over her, slanting his mouth across hers as he slid a hand up her thigh, pushing her dress out of the way as he went.

"You taste delicious," Luke whispered before kissing her again.

"That's the chocolate," she replied, moving her hands up his bare chest and neck until she could bury her fingers in his hair.

"I don't think it is," Kit said. He swept her hair back from her neck and sucked on the skin of her throat.

"More chocolate or more kisses?" Luke asked, his mouth still lightly touching hers.

"Both," she said. *Not just both. Everything.*

"As you wish. Chocolate first."

This time, when he placed the candy in her mouth, she managed to capture his finger between her teeth before he could pull away. She stroked her tongue over his fingertip, sucking on it until she heard him groan. Only then did she release his finger with a pop.

"You're utterly wicked. And I'll have you know you taste delicious even without the chocolate." Kit ran his tongue across the pulse point below her ear as his hands cupped her breasts, his thumbs stroking over her nipples until they tightened into diamond-hard nubs.

Luke whispered her name before kissing her again. This time, he let his tongue sweep into her mouth, savoring her sweet heat. Before the night was over, he wanted to taste every inch of her. She uttered a low moan as he moved his hand higher up the soft plane of her thigh. He didn't stop until his fingers reached the slick lips of her bare pussy. She moaned again as he dipped a finger inside and circled her clit with a slow, deliberate touch.

"You're not wearing underwear. If I had known that, I would've been tempted to skip dinner completely. I want my dessert now, Zura. Can you guess what I want to eat?" Luke asked, his voice barely more than a deep rumble now.

She tightened her fingers in his hair, pulling him in for another kiss as she arched her hips against his fingers.

Kit chuckled and placed an open-mouthed kiss on her neck. "Is that what you want, little one?"

"I know your medi-bots mean you're clean, and so am I. So yes, I want this. All if it. Anything. Just don't you dare stop."

Luke had never heard sweeter words in his life. He kissed her again and managed to ease himself out from beneath her legs. Once he was free, he turned and settled himself between her parted thighs, guiding her legs onto his shoulders.

"Lift your hips," Kit instructed Zura.

She rose up enough for Kit to pull her dress up to her waist, and Luke took a moment to enjoy the view. Zura was lying in Kit's lap, thighs parted, legs bare, and her skin flushed with her arousal.

Kit cradled her in his arms, holding her like the precious treasure they knew her to be. She was achingly beautiful, and the stars seemed to be aligning to make her theirs.

He kissed his way up her inner thigh until he was a mere inch from her pussy. The scent of her arousal flooded his senses, drawing him in until his mouth was on her slick flesh. She moaned, and the sweet sound of her pleasure pushed him beyond his breaking point. He needed this. He needed her, and he would not stop until he heard her scream his name.

Zura was in sensual overload. With Kit's strong hands toying with her breasts and Luke's hot mouth working her clit, her attention bounced from one sensation to the next. She was dizzy with need within seconds, her body responding to their every touch. Weeks of illicit fantasies faded beside the reality of being with both of them, and Zura knew that whatever happened, she would never regret her decision to let them into her life.

"I think this can come off now," Kit murmured between kisses. He released one breast to tug at the blindfold, sliding it over her head with care.

She looked down to see Luke stretched out between her legs, his big hands resting on her thighs. He seemed bigger like this, his body so muscular and solid he could have been carved in stone. He was too perfect to be hers—but he was.

At that moment, Luke looked up. His blue eyes locked on hers, and she couldn't look away. As she watched, he slid a finger inside her, then a second, fucking her with his fingers as he drew her clit into the depths of his mouth and lashed at it with the tip of his tongue.

"I think he likes you watching him. Do you like what you see?" Kit asked, nuzzling her neck.

"Yes. I've never watched—never wanted to. But this? Yes, I like it."

Her words seemed to spur Luke on, and he redoubled his efforts. It all became too much, and before she knew it, she was trembling on the verge of an orgasm. She came with a cry, her eyes closing as her head fell back, her hips rocking, and her inner walls pulsing around Luke's thick fingers.

"I think watching you come is my new favorite pastime," Kit whispered in her ear as she struggled to catch her breath.

"And I have a new favorite dessert," Luke said as he eased himself from between her legs.

"You…I…" She tried to speak, but her thoughts were still too scrambled to form words.

"I rendered our girl speechless." Luke looked utterly smug.

"*We* did, you glory hog. Learn to share," Kit replied.

Zura laughed as her wits slowly returned. "I think you two share very well. If you were any better at it, I'm not sure I'd survive the experience."

Kit cradled her in his arms and knew there wasn't a chance in hell he was letting her go anytime soon. All his good intentions had been blown to atoms the second he pulled her onto his lap. All that was left was a hunger that no food could satisfy.

Luke wiped his mouth with the back of one hand and arched a brow in query. "Care to be shared some more? I should warn you, though. If you say yes, then you're not going to get much sleep tonight."

"I already told you, I'm right where I want to be. That is unless you two want to go somewhere with a bed. Not my room, though. There is no way in hell all three of us would fit comfortably in there."

"Bed later. Right now, I have all I want right here. The only trouble I can see is that you're wearing too many clothes. As much as I love seeing you in that dress, I want to see you out of it even more," Kit said.

Luke stood up and offered Zura his hand. "This would go faster if you actually let go of her, you know."

"How much do you like this dress, little one? Because I'm tempted to tear it off you if it means you'd stay on my lap," Kit said as he tried to figure out a way to get what they all wanted without letting go of Zura.

"If I stay here, you're not going to get out of those clothes. I vote you let me stand up," Zura was laughing as she took Luke's hand and let him help her to her feet.

Luke didn't stop once he had her upright. He tugged her into his arms for another kiss, his hands already busy undoing the fastenings on the back of her dress. By the time Kit rid himself of his shirt, Zura was naked, her clothes lying on the floor at her feet. All she wore was the gold necklace with a battered gold ring hanging between her luscious breasts.

Re'veth, she was breathtaking. He wanted to trace every delicate stripe on her skin and explore every inch of her soft body. Unable to stay away, he found himself moving in behind her so that the soft curve of her ass was pressed against his thighs, and he could feel the satin heat of her skin against his bare chest. She moaned and reached behind her, gripping his thigh with one hand while she held onto Luke's shoulder with the other.

Zura was surrounded by strength and male heat. Every move any of them made produced a delicious friction that only added to the fire already burning inside her. Luke's kisses were passionate and demanding, his hips rocking into hers with every stroke of his tongue. Kit moved in time with his brother until she was swaying between them in an erotic dance.

"I need you, little one. Tell me you're ready for us," Kit whispered.

"I'm ready. I've been dreaming about this for so long," she confessed. Both men went still, and Luke groaned.

"Why didn't you say something?" he asked.

"Because I had convinced myself it was better to be on my own. Because I didn't want to risk our friendship. At first, I wasn't even sure you thought of me that way. Most guys don't. I'm used to it."

"Most guys are idiots, myself included. I admit I didn't notice you at first, but I've been thinking about this since you came to stay with us, and I finally got to know you." Kit kissed her brow in a tender gesture that touched her heart.

"We're here now. That's all that matters," she said, meaning every word.

"Well said," Kit murmured and nuzzled her neck.

"Couch or table?" Luke asked, and it took her a moment to grasp what he was asking.

"I vote for the couch. The table's cold, hard, and covered in dishes at the moment," she said.

"Couch it is." Luke palmed her breasts, teasing her aching nipples.

"Follow Luke. He'll show you where we want you," Kit told her and moved away, freeing her to move.

Luke went quiet for a moment and then grinned. "Oh yeah, that's perfect."

"What's perfect? Are you two talking to each other in your heads? That's totally cheating!" Zura complained as she found herself being led around to the side of the couch.

Luke took her wrists in his hands and placed them on the arm of the sofa. "We were, but only so Kit could explain what he was thinking. As for what's perfect, that would be you, standing like that. Absolute perfection. Don't move."

"Keep in mind that I don't take orders well. That's why I'm the captain of my own ship," she muttered but kept her hands where they were…for now.

Luke chuckled and kissed the curve of her shoulder before moving away again. "That's one of the many reasons I like you, but for now, do as you're told."

She missed the warmth of their bodies surrounding hers. The cooler air of the room made her shiver and sent a wave of goose bumps chasing over her skin. Before she could protest their absence, Luke reappeared, gloriously naked. She drank in the sight of his sculpted body and sizeable cock as he knelt on the couch so that he was facing her. The moment he was settled, he leaned in and kissed her with an all-consuming hunger that rekindled the fire in her blood and made her forget all about being cold.

While her focus was on Luke, Kit moved in behind her, his big hands stroking down her flanks to her hips. He leaned down to press a string of kisses along her spine, then moved one hand from her hip to the slick lips of her pussy. She moaned and arched against his probing fingers while Luke began playing with her breasts again.

"You are so damned sexy," Luke said as he skimmed a fingertip around her areola and flicked the hardened nipple.

"Beautiful," Kit murmured, his breath fanning across her bare skin.

Zura was flying high. They were finally going to be together, and they somehow hadn't even made it to a bedroom, yet.

Kit was enjoying every second of their time with Zura. Seeing her like this, with her naked body glowing with arousal and her voice husky with need, was enough to make him want to keep the damned door locked for a week. Maybe longer. He stroked his fingers through the cream-soaked folds of her pussy, focusing his attention on the swollen nub of her clit. Every touch made her tremble and rock against him, and her responsiveness was making it nearly impossible to think. All he knew was that he hadn't even had her yet, and he was already certain that when this night was over, his life wouldn't be the same.

He leaned over her, wrapping his fingers in the warm silk of her hair and breathing in the scent of her arousal. The way she was bent over put her breasts at the perfect height for his brother to fondle while he kissed her. Watching her with Luke was making it hard for him to remember their plans to go slowly, and Luke had already made it clear he wasn't in the mood to take it easy or slow.

"I need you, Kit. Don't make me wait any longer," Zura said.

Her soft words undid the last of Kit's good intentions, and he shifted his hands back to her hips, coaxing her up on her toes. It only took a few adjustments to find the right angle to bring them together, and then the head of his cock was seated at her entrance. He eased into her an inch at a time, savoring the welcoming heat of her body. She moaned and pushed backward, driving him deeper.

"More!" she demanded.

"Patience. You're so damned tight around my cock it's incredible, but I don't want to hurt you."

"You won't." Zura turned her head to smile at him over her shoulder. "I'm not going to break, I promise."

Kit stared into her eyes and felt something give way deep in his soul. He uttered a wordless groan, and then buried himself balls deep in her body. She moaned in response as her inner walls clamped around his dick.

"Yes!" Her wild cry filled the room.

His brother sealed her mouth with a kiss that muffled her cries as Kit gave free rein to his desires. Even then, her moans were loud enough for Kit to hear her pleasure. He wrapped an arm around her waist so that she was lifted, supported by his forearm. The slight change in angle made it so that his cock stroked over her g-spot with almost every thrust.

Soon, she was trembling in his arms, her fingers sunk deep into the arm of the couch as she braced herself against the pounding rhythm of his hips. Luke groaned, and Kit looked up to find that Zura had taken Luke's cock into her mouth. The sight was almost enough to make him come on the spot. Luke's hands were buried in Zura's hair, and his head was thrown back in ecstasy as he worked his shaft between her lips.

Kit's strokes grew more erratic, his pace accelerating as his orgasm grew imminent. Aware that Zura hadn't reached hers yet, he shifted his hand so that he could reach between her legs and press the pad of his index finger hard against her clit, trapping it against her pubic bone. She stiffened, shuddering as the new contact pushed her closer to her breaking point.

The sounds of sex and pleasure filled the room as the three of them soared together. When Zura came, she started a chain reaction. The pulsing grip of her inner walls triggered Kit's release, and moments later Luke shuddered and withdrew from Zura's mouth, fisting his cock hard to stave off his orgasm.

Zura had to take a few deep breaths before she could speak again. "Wow," she finally managed to murmur as she relaxed her death grip on the arm of the couch and lifted her head.

"What she said," Luke groaned.

"Why didn't you finish?" she asked Luke.

He flashed a sultry smile that made her pulse race yet again. "Because, gorgeous, I want to be inside you when that happens. I just wasn't expecting you to be so damned talented with that tongue of yours. You nearly broke me."

Kit eased her back down so that she was standing squarely on the ground and then he withdrew from her with a contented sigh. "Addictive. That's what you are. Beautiful, sexy, and very damned addictive."

"You two are going to give me a swollen head the way you compliment me. It's sweet, but it's not necessary."

Kit swatted her ass just hard enough to sting a little. "Stop that. That's the second time you've tried to deflect a compliment. I know what I'm saying, little one, and I mean every damned word."

"Did you just spank me?" she asked, straightening up despite the fact her legs were still shaking from the mind blowing orgasm Kit had given her.

"I do believe he did," Luke said with a snicker.

Kit arched a dark brow and stared down at her without a hint of remorse in his expression. "I did, and I'll do it as many times as it takes for you to understand that we think you are beautiful and sexy and amazing."

She didn't know whether to be amused, indignant, or furious, and somehow ended up being all three at once. "Are all cyborg men this arrogant and pushy?"

"Yes," both brothers answered in the same breath.

"Awesome," she muttered under her breath.

"If you're done distracting our girl now, Kit, I'd like to get back to what we were doing a minute ago. Zura, my beauty, come here." Luke had moved to the center of the couch, but was still on his knees, facing her, and he patted the spot directly in front of him.

Kit didn't give her a chance to move on her own. He scooped her into his arms, lifted her over the arm of the couch, and into Luke's waiting embrace.

"Thank you, my brother," Luke almost purred with satisfaction as he settled her so that she was sitting on his lap, her weight on his thighs and her legs wrapped around his waist.

"I could have walked," she protested.

"Our way was faster. We've wasted enough time getting to this point. I don't want to waste another second. I want you. Now. Tell me you want that, too," Luke murmured.

"So much it scares me," she confessed and kissed him. He groaned and kissed her, his tongue sliding into her mouth to tease and taste. His cock was a steel-hard rod pressed against the lips of her pussy, and she could feel it swell and thicken the moment her lips touched his.

"There's nothing to be scared of," Kit said from somewhere behind her.

She knew that wasn't true. If this didn't work out, she would be losing two friends, and her heart might never recover.

Please, let this work.

Luke's kisses were demanding and fiery, and there was no denying the passion that blazed between them. His arms tensed as he lifted her a few inches, shifting their bodies so that his cock was lying between her labia. When he moved her again, it was to slide her along his hard length. Her clit throbbed against the pressure of his cock as he stroked through her folds. A low, rumbling groan rose from his chest, and she knew he was feeling the same delicious torment she was. She wrapped her arms around his neck and used him to leverage herself a little higher. She wanted him inside her.

"No more teasing," she whispered against his lips.

"No more waiting," he replied, bringing their bodies together so that the thick head of his cock stroked along her clitoris one last time before sliding into her channel.

"Finally," Luke spoke so softly that she barely caught what he said.

"And whose fault is that?" she asked, teasing him.

Kit burst out laughing, and she turned her head to find him still naked and watching them from a chair at the table they had abandoned.

"It was his fault, gorgeous. I knew what I wanted a while ago, but I had to wait for Kit to figure it out for himself," Luke replied before dropping his head to the crook of her neck and nipping her throat sharply.

The brief bite of pain made her pussy clench around his cock, and he groaned in approval. He buried his face against her throat, muttering something she couldn't quite hear as he drove himself deep into her body.

Luke was battling to stay in control, and it was a fight he was losing. He had nearly bitten Zura hard enough to leave a mark, and some dark corner of his psyche was still demanding he do just that. Mark her. Brand her so that no other male would dare to look at what was his.

Her skin was glowing and flushed with passion, her lovely eyes closed as she worked her body over his. Her inner walls milked his dick with every move she made, and he knew it wouldn't be long before he came. He shifted her in his arms, loosening his hold so that the angle between them opened a few degrees. The moment he moved, Zura's eyes flew open, and she moaned. Her legs tightened around him and a soft shudder rolled through her body as he hit her g-spot again.

"Yesss," she moaned again.

"Touch yourself, Zura. I want to watch you come before I do. I want to feel you coming around my dick."

"I figured Kit would be the bossy one," she muttered.

"Same software, remember? We're both bossy. Get used to it."

"I'm only doing this because it's a good idea," she retorted before unwinding one arm from around his neck and slipping it between their bodies to where they were joined.

The added pressure of her fingers against his shaft made his balls tighten, and his control slipped another notch. There was enough space between them for him to see everything as she rode him, her breasts bouncing slightly in time to the rocking of their bodies. Her skin color intensified, her stripes darkening even as her eyes gleamed like molten silver. Every breath grew more ragged and uneven as she neared her climax. He couldn't tear his eyes away from the vision she presented. Wild, passionate, and beautiful, she rode him hard as she took what she needed.

Watching her reach her climax was more intoxicating than the finest liquor. She threw back her head and cried out his name as she came, her body arching against his as she came apart in his arms. Knowing she had found her release, he finally gave into his own. He switched their positions, lowering her to the couch so that he was on top of her, his body pinning hers down as he took her hard and fast.

She released her legs from his waist, freeing him to move even faster, and it wasn't long before he found his own release, emptying himself inside her until he felt as though he was being turned inside out. He was still regaining his senses when Zura started to giggle beneath him.

"What?" he asked.

"I'm trying to figure out what we're going to tell your sister when she asks what happened to the couch in here."

"Huh?" Luke had no idea what she was talking about until he started to look around. At some point after he pinned her down, he must have lost control, because the cushion was now crushed and mangled where his left hand had been. He had gripped it too tightly, destroying it.

"You ever notice how most of the furniture in the club is the same from room to room?" Kit asked.

"Not really. Is it?"

Luke grinned at her. "Oh yeah. There's a reason for that. It saves on replacement costs when you order in bulk. Out here in the Drift, damage happens."

"Regularly," Kit agreed.

"Do you lose control like that often? I'm starting to wonder what I've gotten myself into here," she said, laughing the whole time.

"Only with you," both of them answered at once, sending her into another gale of laughter.

"You're really adorable when you do that, you know," she told them when she had the breath to speak.

"That's no way to talk to the man who just made you scream his name," Luke grumbled playfully.

She stuck her tongue out at him and wriggled a little. "You're my men; I can call you whatever I want."

"Your men. I like the sound of that," he said as he kissed her and withdrew from her body with care.

"I do, too," she said and sat up.

"I think it's time we took this to another room. One with a shower and a big, soft bed," Kit announced.

"Tell me your rooms aren't far away. The last thing I want is to get caught sneaking down the hall looking like I was part of an orgy." She raked a hand through her disheveled hair and laughed. "I'm pretty sure that's exactly what I look like at the moment."

"You look sexy as hell and very debauched. It's a good look for you," Luke told her as he rose to his feet and started hunting for his clothes. He would put them on only as long as it took to make the walk back to Kit's quarters, which were the closest to where they were right now. The moment they were through that door, he planned on getting naked again and staying that way for the rest of the night.

Maybe they would keep Zura naked and in bed all day tomorrow, too. They might have been slow to make their move, but now they had, he wasn't going to let her stray far from his side or their bed.

CHAPTER SIX

Zura tucked the last of her things into her bag and slipped the strap over her shoulder. In her hand was the keycard Kit and Luke had given her two nights before. It struck her that this place, and the key she held, represented something she had never considered the first time she set foot inside the club. The club had become a second home to her, a place where she felt like she truly belonged. It had been a gradual change, but there wasn't any way she could deny it any longer.

She was going to miss this place while she was gone. The club, and everyone in it, especially two arrogant, sexy-as-hell brothers who had recently tilted her world on its axis.

Zura left her room and made her way to the elevator. She had a job to do, and to do it she needed to get back to the *Sun Sprite*. Once she was back from this run, the three of them were going to have to talk about how this relationship was going to work. She had come out here to start over and forge a new life for herself, a simple life. The last thing she had expected was to wind up dating a pair of cyborgs.

So much for simple.

The elevator door opened on the main level, and instead of the empty hallway she was expecting, she found herself face to face with her lovers. They were standing shoulder to shoulder, blocking the corridor completely.

"Come to say goodbye?" she asked, pleased to see them again.

"Not exactly," Luke said with a hint of a grin.

"You can't keep me here. If that's your plan, forget it. I'm due to leave in two hours, and I don't plan on being late."

"You're cute when you get all feisty, little one. We're not here to try and stop you. Luke is here to say goodbye, and I'm here because I'm going with you," Kit said.

He stated it with such casualness, it took her a moment to register what he was saying, but then she noticed that he had a bag packed and slung over one shoulder.

"You're coming with me? How's that going to work? You're needed here." Zura was torn. Part of her was rejoicing that they cared enough about her to want to watch her back, even while she was away from the Drift. Another part of her chafed at the idea of having someone else aboard her ship, particularly a certain arrogant, pushy cyborg who had announced he was going with her on a run instead of asking.

"Nope, we're kicking him out." Cyn appeared in the hallway behind the two men. "He needs to get away from here for a few days, and as it happens, you're going in that direction."

Zura scoffed. "Since when is 'away from here' a direction?"

Kit chuckled. "My place is with you. You're not going out there alone this time, Zura. You need someone to watch your back, and I'm volunteering for the job."

"You've never taken so much as a day off in all the time I've known you. Are you sure about this?"

He folded his arms across his chest and gave her a stern look that made her pulse kick up a couple of notches. It wasn't fair that he looked so damned sexy when he went into full commander mode.

"We're not going to the far end of the cosmos; you said it was a short run to a restock station. We'll be back in less than a week. It's been pointed out to me by my business partners that I have them, along with a well-trained and fully capable staff, who can take care of the club while I'm gone. You have no one, Zura. Therefore, I'm coming with you." He paused, and his lips quirked into a ghost of a smile. "Please?"

And there it was. He said please. A little late, but he was still making an effort. Zura knew it wasn't in Kit's nature to ask permission for anything. "Are you traveling as crew or cargo?"

"Crew. For the duration of this flight, I'm your security officer and bodyguard."

She grinned. "Then this is going to be fun. I have to be polite to passengers, but if you're crew, then that means I'm your commanding officer." She lifted her bag from her shoulder and handed it to him. "Carry this for me, crewman."

Kit took it from her with without missing a beat. "Yes, Captain Watson."

Cyn snickered. "I knew I liked you, Zura. Come back safely and have a good trip."

"Captain? Oh man. I'm sorry I'm going to miss this." Luke was laughing as he gathered her into his arms for a slow, lingering kiss that sent shockwaves racing through her.

"Behave yourself while I'm gone," she told him when he finally ended their kiss.

"I will. I'll see you in a few days, gorgeous." Luke looked up to meet his brother's eyes. "Take care of our girl."

"You know I will," Kit replied.

Luke kissed her brow and finally released her from the confines of his arms as he muttered, "I hate goodbyes."

"You better get used to them, sexy. You know what my life is like. I'll be back before you know it." Zura felt another unfamiliar pang of regret at having to leave. It was a strange feeling. She was raised as a vagabond, always on the move. The only home she had ever known was the *Sun Sprite*. Having a second home and leaving someone she cared about behind was all uncharted territory.

"Next time, I'll go with you, and Kit can stay here. Deal?" Luke asked.

His offer made her happier than it should have considering how much she valued her privacy and quiet time on the *Sun Sprite*. "Maybe. Wait and see how Kit fares. Odds are good he'll be bored out of his mind and so would you."

He winked at her. "I doubt that. I can think of all sorts of things we could be doing to pass the time."

Kit moved in behind her, one arm slipping around her waist. "I'll let you know what we come up with. You'll just have to wait until next time."

"And on that note, we need to get going. I still need to double-check the manifest, sign off on the paperwork, and apparently, I need to tell my ship's AI there's a new crewman on board."

"You have to log me in with the ship's computer?" Kit asked.

"Well, I could skip that step, but I don't think you'd enjoy what would happen. No registration means no access to the computer, the food supplies, or the ability to open any door on the ship."

Kit nodded in approval. "Then by all means, log me in. I like the set-up, though. I want to see all you can show me about your current security system. There might be a few things I can tweak for you, and I'll probably learn a few things along the way."

"Damn right you're going to learn a few things. If you want to be my security officer, then you've got a lot to learn. You've been retired for years, but I bet you still know your way around weaponry, so we'll start by teaching you how to man the ship's guns."

"He gets to shoot things? Oh man, I'm jealous," Luke sulked.

"Frankly, so am I," Cyn agreed. "I don't suppose we could outfit the club with a few lasers, or maybe a wide beam neural disruptor for rough nights…"

"I know that look. Forget it, Cynder. Whatever you're thinking of, it's not happening. I'll see you two when I get back, and do not install any weapons while I'm gone." Kit waved at the others before leading the way out through the main door and into the bar.

He was leaving. More than that, he was about to leave Luke and Cyn behind and go off without them. It was a strange feeling, one Kit was still wrapping his head around as they left the club behind them and headed across the main concourse. He slowed for a moment to look back over his shoulder.

"Have you ever been separated from him before?" Zura asked.

"Not like this, no. We've been on different parts of a battlefield, and occasionally one of us has been planetside while the other one was in orbit, but we've rarely been apart since the day we were pulled out of our maturation tank. We were created to work together, two halves of a whole. This will be the first time we've been far enough apart that our internal comm link won't work. It's going to be a little strange. Quiet though. I'm looking forward to the quiet."

"You don't have to come with me, Kit."

"Yes, I do," he said simply. It was the truth.

She rolled her eyes at him and took his hand before walking toward the docking ring. "I can take care of myself. The *Sun Sprite* is my home; I'll be perfectly safe on board."

"This isn't about you, Zura. This is for me—and Luke, too. We couldn't let you go alone. It's not who we are. You're too important to me. To both of us."

Her answering smile lit up her face. "It's the same for me, but I think we're probably worried about nothing. Whatever it is Vin wants from me, he's not going to get it. Eventually, he'll figure that out and go away again. I'm never going back to him, or that life. I'm happy where I am."

"I'm glad to hear it. We're happier now you're here, too. Besides, I can't see you as a smuggler. You have too much compassion. If you didn't, you wouldn't have risked your life to bring that vaccine back. You're not the kind to risk dying purely for profit."

She nodded and touched the ring she kept on a chain around her neck. "My father was always saying that luck was a poor man's only insurance policy. His luck ran out far too soon, and I don't want to wind up like him. That's why I wear this. He said it was his good luck charm. It's to remind me not to take foolish chances... at least, not too many."

"You mean like taking up with a couple of cyborgs way the hell out here on the dark side of beyond?" he asked.

"Something like that. My father had another saying that I think applies in this case. No risk, no reward."

They reached the doorway to her ship. She opened the hatch with a wave of her hand over the access panel before glancing up at him. "You ready, Crewman Armas?"

"I'm ready. In fact, I'm looking forward to it. Part of our batch's programming included a directive that all the others look to Luke and me for leadership. Even Luke is programmed to defer to me if it's required. It'll be nice to relinquish command for a few days."

"We'll see if you still feel that way by the time we're back home."

She stepped inside, still holding his hand, and he followed, ducking his head to avoid the pipes and conduits that ran along the ceiling. He would need to remember to keep his head low, or he was going to have a damned concussion by the time they got back.

He glanced around his new home for the next few days. There was no doubt that this was a working ship and not a luxury vessel. The deck plates were worn, and the walls bore countless scratches and dents. It all felt familiar to him, though. He had traveled on countless ships not that different from this one over the years. The *Sun Sprite* was smaller, but that was really the only difference.

A closer look showed him that despite its well-used appearance, the *Sun Sprite* was in good repair, at least to Kit's eyes. He had been a passenger on far worse ships with frayed wires sparking overhead, while the pipes dripped coolant and released random bursts of steam into the corridors. The corporations hadn't worried much about their cyborg soldier's comforts. So long as they were fed, armed, and ready to fight, that was all that mattered.

"C'mon. I'll take you to my, uh, our quarters. Once our stuff is stowed away, we'll need to hit the cargo bay and get to work. I'll give you a proper tour once we're on our way."

"Sounds good to me." He ducked his head and fell in behind her. That was the other reason he had readily agreed to go with Zura on this run. The opportunity to spend time with her, just the two of them, was too good to refuse. If things worked out the way he hoped, then the three of them would be together for a long time. Maybe even a lifetime. Time alone with her would be precious, and he intended to take advantage of every chance he got to be in Zura's company.

CHAPTER SEVEN

By the time they handed over control of her ship to the computer for the night, Kit was pleasantly tired. True to her word, Zura had treated him as a member of her crew, and he now had a better understanding, as well as a healthy respect, for what she did for a living. Once the cargo was confirmed and their destination set, Kit assumed the work was done. He had been wrong.

Before they even left the dock, she had run diagnostics, calculated fuel consumption, repaired a minor malfunction in one of the air recycling systems, and raced the length and breadth of the ship countless times, making sure that everything was squared away and running smoothly. He shadowed her every step of the way, learning what he could as they went.

Once they were under way, she started teaching him about her ship's security and defense set up, and he had spent hours learning the *Sun Sprite*'s complex systems and running simulated scenarios. He hadn't actually gotten to blow anything up, but it had been a hell of a lot of fun pretending he was. Zura hadn't been joking when she'd said she was capable of defending herself. The *Sun Sprite* was fast, agile, well shielded, and even better armed.

It reminded him of his days as a soldier, only Zura was a far kinder commander than any other he ever served with, himself included.

With the ship's computer handling the ship for the night shift, he had risen from his seat and followed her down the corridor to her quarters. The bed was actually bigger than he was prepared for. There was plenty of room for them both, though fitting all three of them on it would have been a challenge. Not that he expected that would be a problem they would have very often. Zura's life might be on the *Sun Sprite*, but his and Luke's was back on the Drift. While one of them could travel with her, it would affect the running of the club if both of them were gone for long periods of time.

Zura moved to her side of the cabin and started to strip out of her clothes. "Any regrets about coming along? I know my ship isn't nearly as comfortable as your club."

"No regrets. I'd sleep on the floor with a rock for a pillow if it meant I could keep you safe. Instead, I'm sharing your bed and learning more about you and your life. This is no hardship, little one."

"It's not much of a vacation, either. First a soldier, then a business owner. Have you ever taken time off for yourself?" She dropped her clothes into the laundry chute to be cleaned overnight, and slipped into bed, still naked.

"Time off? Not really, no. You know what it's like when you are part of a family business and your workplace is also your home. I bet you've never taken time off, either."

Zura laughed and snuggled into her bed, happy to be back onboard again. She was even happier to have Kit with her. So far, having him on board had been fun, and for once, she hadn't been lonely. "You'd win that bet. My dad took me on day trips sometimes if there was time, but there are some planets I've visited dozens of times and never seen more than a few blocks away from the spaceport. Maybe one day, when I've got enough money saved up to start feeling like my future's secure, I'll take a real vacation."

"If that day ever comes, maybe I'll go with you."

He peeled off his clothes, giving her a glorious view of his naked body before climbing into bed with her. He took up every inch of extra room, and Zura knew there was no way the three of them would ever fit the way things were. She would have to think about how to rectify that. If this worked out, that is. If this whole relationship wasn't going to crash and burn someday soon.

"I thought you said you had better things to do than lounge around on a vacation?" she asked.

He grunted and pulled her into his arms before answering. "As my family has been pointing out to me recently, we can't work every hour of every day. I'm entitled to have a life, too. I may have lost track of that idea of late, but that doesn't make it any less true."

Zura knew what it must be costing Kit to make that confession, and it made her like him all the more. "It might be that I've been doing the same thing. When Dad was alive, we were always chasing down jobs and scrambling to make ends meet. Once he was gone, I kept doing what we had always done. It never occurred to me to do anything else."

"The family business was all you knew, so you kept doing it. I get it." He reached back to rearrange his pillow, then frowned in confusion.

"What?" she asked, only belatedly realizing what he must have found. He pulled his hand out from beneath the pillow and held up the palm-sized pleasure toy she had forgotten about.

"What's this, a weapon?"

She groaned and silently hoped for a rogue comet to sideswipe them and save her from any explanation. "That's not a weapon. It's uh... personal. Hand it over and pretend you never saw that, please."

"Personal?" He turned it over and then started to chuckle as he realized what he was holding.

"Give. Now." She held out her hand to him.

"Nope. I have a better idea. I want to watch you use it."

The look he gave her had her brain melting around the edges and her breath catching in her throat. He wanted to watch?

"Why would I want to use that when I have you here? Trust me, there's no comparison."

"I'm glad to hear it. I still want you to use it on yourself. I've always wondered what women do when they're alone." He propped himself up on one elbow and held out the toy to her.

"You've never watched a woman do that before?" Zura assumed there wasn't much her guys hadn't done in their lives. The idea of being able to share something new with Kit was appealing enough to help her overcome her initial shyness.

"Never. I'm no saint. Not even close, but until we were released from service there wasn't much time for that sort of thing. Since then, there have been a few brief flings and well, Andrea, and you know how that went."

She nodded. "It went about as well as my relationship with Vin, and they both ended in a fiery wreck. I'm hoping to avoid that this time around."

"Me too." Kit brushed his knuckles across her cheek in a tender gesture that filled her with a warmth that had nothing to do with desire. "I want to get to know who you are and how our lives could come together, Zura. I want this to last."

She blew out a soft breath and smiled. "I'm not sure how we're going to make this work, but I want this to last, too."

His smile made her heart sing. "We'll figure it out, together." Then he held up her toy, and his smile turned into a wicked grin. "Now…How about showing me how this works. When I'm back on the station, and you're off on a run without me, I'd like to be able to close my eyes and think about you doing this while I'm not there to please you myself."

Desire and something stronger bloomed deep in her heart, swelling with every word he spoke. "And Luke said you sucked at seduction and romance."

Kit laughed as she threw off the blankets, letting him see what she was doing. If she was going to do this, then she was going to give him a show he would never forget. She took the toy and settled it into her hand before placing her feet flat on the bed and spreading her legs wide. With her free hand, she reached between her thighs and parted her lower lips, working her clit with her forefinger.

A low groan had her looking over at Kit, who was staring at her with hungry eyes. "So damned sexy. Keep going. Tell me what you'd do if you were here alone."

"If I were out here alone, I would turn off the lights, close my eyes, and fantasize about the two sexiest men I've ever seen. Big, strong, identical twins who would do all sorts of wicked things to me. That's what I used to do, anyway. Now, I don't have to fantasize anymore. I can close my eyes and think back to all the things we've done together and all the things we're going to do."

"You thought about us?" Kit asked, his voice dropping to barely more than a rough whisper.

"I did. Almost every night, lying in this bed, alone." She flicked her fingers across her aching clit, teasing herself.

"Show me what you'd do when you thought about me," he ordered.

"I'd take this and put it up against my clitoris. Then I'd turn it to the lowest setting. That gets the vibrations started, and it sucks real gently on my clit." She put the toy in place and turned it on. She was already so turned on that even the lowest setting made her toes curl. Within seconds, her pussy was soaked, and her clit was throbbing in time to the pulsing vibrations directed at it, and she couldn't hold back a soft moan.

"*Fraxx.* That's the hottest thing I've ever seen. Don't stop. Tell me what you'd do next."

Kit couldn't tear his eyes off Zura. Her hair was fanned out over her pillow, and her beautiful body was stretched out beside him, tempting him to touch her. The pattern of blue lines that marked her skin was darkening more every second, and her eyes were trained on him. The low hum of her toy was a steady counterpoint to the soft, breathy moans and sighs that spilled from her lips as she pleasured herself.

"Next, I would turn up the power. Sometimes slowly, sometimes all at once. Depends on my mood."

"Do it." He threw back the blankets that covered him and wrapped his fist around his cock. It was the only way he could stop himself from reaching for her. He would need to have her soon, but not yet. He wanted to watch her a little longer, first.

The tip of her tongue swiped over her lower lip as she watched him stroke his cock. "No ordering me around on my own ship. You want this, ask nicely."

He chuckled, turned on even more by her small act of defiance. "Please, little one. Come for me."

"I thought you'd never ask."

She moved her fingers, and the low hum of her toy grew louder, then louder still. Within seconds, she was moaning, her eyes glazing over as she writhed beside him. Her free hand came up to cover her breast, and she began playing with her nipple, pinching and rolling it between her fingers. He continued to watch, stroking himself as she lost herself in the pleasure of the moment. When her thighs were trembling and her every breath was a ragged gasp, he leaned over her, caressing her hand with his before plunging two fingers into the tight heat of her channel.

"Kit!" She cried out his name as her hips rose from the mattress.

She was so close to release that it only took a few pumps of his hand to push her over the edge. Her inner walls flexed tightly against his fingers as she came hard and fast.

"Beautiful," he whispered before kissing her.

She uttered a breathless laugh as she tossed the toy aside and wrapped her arms around his shoulders. Nails raked lightly over his skin, and her answering kiss was full of hunger. She lowered her legs and slid under his body, pulling him into place over her, until their bodies were aligned and he was between her thighs.

"That was fun, but I'd rather have you than any toy. You're real, and you're here, and I want to be with you. I can go back to toys when my bed is empty again."

"Maybe next time, Luke can go with you. We'll find a way to make this work, Zura."

"There'll be times I'll have to go without either of you. You know that. It's okay, though. I'm used to being on my own. At least, for now, I have the two of you to come back to."

For one brief moment, her guard dropped, letting him see a glimpse of her vulnerable side. This was a part of her he had never seen before. Seeing her like that, staring up at him with eyes soft with hope and shadowed with past pain was enough to send his protective instincts into orbit. "Yes, you do."

He leaned in and kissed her with so much heat that it should have left scorch marks on the sheets. She twined one leg around his hips and arched upward, bringing their bodies together as their tongues dueled, and his world went up like a supernova. He drove into her body without slowing. He needed to be buried inside her, to feel her heat wrapped around him like silk and fire.

Wild need coursed through him, and for the first time, he stopped holding himself back. He needed to possess her completely. She was the woman he had dreamed of all those long, lonely nights he had been a soldier. Warm and compassionate, but brave too. She didn't care that he was part machine; to her, he was a man. She was his perfect match, and at that moment, he knew with stunning clarity that he would never let her go.

Zura let herself get lost in the moment. Nothing existed beyond herself, Kit, and the passion that burned between them. She was the center of his world, and he was the center of hers. It was the most amazing feeling in the world, and she never wanted it to end.

He moved over her with pounding force. Every hard thrust and bruising kiss made her soar higher. When he tore his mouth from hers to bury his face into the side of her neck, she could feel his teeth pressed to her throat in a love bite she knew would leave a mark for days to come.

The thought only made the fire in her heart burn brighter.

Their sweat-slicked bodies danced together for a while longer, drawing out every moment of pleasure. When the end came, it took them both together in a shockwave of bliss that sent them spinning out of control. There were still stars dancing behind her eyelids when her senses returned and she found herself pinned beneath the still-panting bulk of her cyborg lover.

"I think you broke me," she said as she opened her eyes to find him smiling down at her.

"Better than your toy?"

"Infinitely better. If you ever get tired of running the Nova, you can move onto the *Sun Sprite* and be my personal sex toy."

Kit froze. "What did you say?"

"I was teasing you, but something tells me I said something wrong," she said, reaching up to cradle his face in her hands. His expression was stony, and there were shadows in his eyes that hadn't been there only seconds before.

The silence stretched out between them, but finally Kit sighed. "You didn't say anything wrong. You just…that's what Andrea called us. The night we asked her to move in with us, she laughed and said she wasn't some pathetic fool who was going to fall for her sex toys. That's all we were to her:

toys. Machines she could play with and then toss aside when she was done."

"She said what? That bitch deserves to get her ass fired into the nearest star. Maybe a black hole. You're not machines. Well, I mean, you sort of are, but that's not *who* you are. You're so much more than that, Kit."

His expression softened a little at a time, until the storms were gone from his eyes, and he was smiling again. "I'm such a fool. I wasted so much time twisted up in knots over her when I should have been seeing what was right in front of me. *Fraxx*, I should have listened to Luke. Please, don't ever tell him I said that, though."

"It can be our little secret," she promised him, while making another promise to herself. If she ever crossed paths with Andrea, she was going to tear her to pieces for what she had done.

Kit didn't say a word; he simply held her tight.

Lying there, wrapped up in her lover's arms, Zura felt more at peace than she had in years. She didn't know how the hell she was going to make it work, but some time in the last few days, Kit and Luke had become something worth fighting for. If they weren't planning on letting go, then neither was she.

* * * *

Two nights later, they were speaking with Luke over the ship's video comms. They talked for a few minutes every night. So far there hadn't been anything of importance to relay, but Zura was enjoying their nightly chats. It was the first time she had ever had a reason to keep in contact with someone like this.

"So, how do you like the trip so far?" Luke asked.

"I'm enjoying it, especially the peace and quiet. No annoying siblings around to ruin my good mood," Kit retorted. He was sitting in the ship's mess with Zura on his lap as they chatted with Luke on the monitor.

"We don't miss you, either. The place seems positively sunny without your broody, grumpy ass stomping around. Zura, feel free to leave him at the resupply station and come back alone. I miss you, gorgeous."

She blew him a kiss. "I miss you, too."

"Don't worry. I'm taking good care of her." Kit leaned down and kissed her. It was a long, slow, seductive kiss that melted her brain, made her instantly wet, and left her wanting more.

"You're a total bastard."

Kit chuckled and lifted his head to grin at his brother's image on the monitor. "You say that like it's a new discovery for you."

"Fine, you're being even more of a bastard than usual. I swear, Zura, next time, I'm coming with you, and Kit can stay behind to babysit the club."

Kit slid a hand down the front of her shirt and kissed her again. "Yeah. Next time. This time, she's all mine. Say good night, Luke. It's time I tucked our girl into bed."

"Asshole. You're going to pay for this when you get back," Luke grumbled.

"We'll be back soon enough, sexy, then we can make up for lost time," Zura promised. She was enjoying her time away with Kit, but that didn't stop her from missing Luke at the same time.

"Good night, gorgeous. I'll see you in my dreams," Luke said to her, then looked at Kit. "And you, I'll see in my nightmares. Have a good night, you two."

"You, too," she said.

"Night, Luke."

The link was severed, and the screen went blank.

"You shouldn't tease him that way; it was mean," she scolded Kit. She was trying to ignore the way his fingers were toying with her nipple, but with every passing second, she was growing more aroused.

"I'll never stop teasing him. If I did, he'd think I was malfunctioning or something."

"Well, we can't have that." She leaned in and kissed him hungrily.

"Now, I'm going to take you to bed and tease you a little, too. Maybe a lot. I wouldn't want you to feel left out."

Kit scooped her into his arms and kissed her again before rising and heading for her quarters.

One thing she knew for certain: With both Kit and Luke in her life, she was never likely to feel left out of anything again.

CHAPTER EIGHT

Kit was squeezed into the co-pilot's seat in the cockpit of the *Sun Sprite*. It wasn't built with cyborgs in mind, but it was worth a little discomfort to be able to watch as Zura deftly navigated the ship to their assigned berth and set her down with a practiced hand.

"Welcome to Resupply Station Fargo. We'll have a few hours of downtime while we refuel and offload the cargo and then we'll head home."

"You do this often? Come and go the same day?" After three days aboard, he was more than ready to get off the *Sun Sprite* and enjoy a change of scenery.

"It depends on where I am. Some places I'll grab a good meal and enjoy myself. If I'm on a resupply station, I usually turn and burn instead of sticking around. Most of them are best described as somewhere between rustic and rusting. The food's all from dispensers, the drinks are criminally watered down, and the only other living beings on the whole station are miners with the bad luck to run out of something they needed before they were due to come back to the Drift. The markup on goods out here is insane. You'll see what I mean when we get inside."

"I've heard about these automated stations. Never been to one, though. Everything is controlled by a single AI and the work's all done by droids and drones, right? It's a little creepy, if you ask me."

"Try being the only person on the whole damned station. That moves the dial from a little creepy to *fraxxing* unnerving real quick." She gestured out the window to where two mining ships and another freighter were docked. "That won't be an issue today."

She rose from her chair and checked the slender data tablet she had carried with her everywhere since coming onboard. "The station's AI has already sent our paperwork. Let's find out where we are on the schedule and how long before we can take off again."

"Yes, captain."

Zura grinned at him. "I really do love it when you say that."

By the time she had completed the requisite paperwork in triplicate and overseen the removal of her cargo, Zura was hungry enough that even a meal at the station's sole eatery sounded good.

Normally she avoided socializing on these trips because a crew of horny miners who hadn't seen a female of any species for months were far from ideal dinner companions. They'd hit on anything with a pulse and didn't respond well to the word 'no' unless it came accompanied by threats of bodily harm.

She was betting that Kit's presence would be enough of a deterrent for them to get through dinner.

She gave Kit a brief tour of the place, but it didn't take long. Mostly it was an excuse for both of them to stretch their legs.

She walked Kit through the cargo bays and refueling area and then made their way to the far end of the station where the computerized commissaries stood ready to dispense everything from toothpaste, to shield amplifiers, to medical supplies.

They were almost done with their tour when Kit reached for her hand, closing his fingers around hers as he muttered something low in his throat.

"What's wrong?"

"Those guys have been staring at you since we came into view." He nodded ahead of them, down the dingy corridor to where several men were standing.

"They don't mean anything by it. I'm probably the first woman they've seen in months. I just ignore them."

"It's rude."

She laughed. "Have you met most of the people on the Drift? It's not like it's populated with charm school graduates."

"It's still *fraxxing* rude to stare. Especially at another man's woman." He drew her in closer to his side.

Was he actually jealous? The idea made her laugh.

Instead of laughing with her, Kit pulled her into his arms and kissed her right there in the middle of the corridor.

His mouth was hard against hers as he plundered her lips. He gripped her hips and lifted her off her feet, taking the kiss deeper as he spun her around and walked her backward until she was up against the dented wall of the station. His hard body pressed against hers, letting her feel every muscled inch of him as he claimed her mouth in one torrid kiss after another. When she felt like she was standing in the center of a star, he finally tore his mouth from hers.

"What was that for?" she asked in a dazed whisper.

"Because I wanted to let those assholes know you're off limits. Do I need another reason?"

Kit's eyes were full of heat as he looked at her.

She cocked her head to one side and pretended to consider her answer for a second before shaking her head. "Nope, you don't."

"In that case, expect me to do that often. You're mine, little one, and I want everyone to know it."

Her heart did a slow somersault in her chest. "If you keep saying things like that, you might get your wish."

"*Fraxx*, I hope so." He kept his hand on the small of her back as they walked the short distance to their destination. The moment he set eyes on the entrance to the self-serve eatery, Kit wondered if they might be better off back on the *Sun Sprite*.

The sign was only partially lit, and several of the letters were flickering. Inside, things weren't any better. The floor was sticky under his feet, the tables were stained and chipped, and the chairs looked like they'd been left in the path of a meteor swarm. The lighting was dim, but he couldn't tell if that was an aesthetic choice or simply a lack of maintenance.

An entire wall was filled with food and drink dispensers, offering a wide array of meal choices, apparently organized by their planet of origin. The signs on the machines were scratched and faded almost beyond recognition. Some of the wording was so damaged that despite the fact his programming allowed him to speak and comprehend every major language known, he didn't recognize one in three words he tried to read, even the ones in Galactic Standard. It was a wonder that the station's visitors didn't poison themselves regularly simply by eating the wrong damn thing.

"How many languages can you read?" he asked as she led him past the Torski and Jeskyran areas to the human options.

"A few. I know a little of everything, really, though Galactic Standard is the only language I speak fluently," she said, then frowned. "Don't tell me you've got a program for languages. If you say yes, I'm going to be jealous."

"Be jealous, then. I think it's your turn, anyway," he said, watching her blush as he reminded her of his jealous kiss in the corridor earlier.

He glanced around to the handful of others who were eating and talking at various points around the place. "You sure it's safe to eat anything here?"

"Is the big, badass cyborg worried about food poisoning?" she asked, laughing as she made her selection.

He ordered the same thing she did just to be safe, and within minutes they were both seated at an empty booth while he tried not to think about how much the meal had cost him. Zura hadn't been kidding about the markup.

She seemed to be spending a lot of time looking around as they tucked into their meal, and Kit got curious. "Who or what are you looking for?"

"I thought I recognized a ship on our way in. If I'm right, then it's someone I knew back when my dad was still alive."

"An old friend? I thought you didn't have any friends out here?"

"I didn't think I did. If Phyl's out this way, then she hasn't been here long. Maybe she'll be able to tell me what Vin wants with me."

"If she knows that, why didn't you contact her when you were talking to your other connections?" he asked.

"I couldn't. She blocked all incoming transmissions from my ship a long time ago."

"Why would she block communications from your ship? Is this a friend or an enemy?"

"She's a friend. It's just that she and my father…let's say they have a past, and she isn't one to forgive, or forget."

"Your father had a knack for pissing people off, didn't he?"

Before Zura could answer, a new voice joined the conversation from the booth behind Zura.

"Russ Watson was one of the biggest assholes in the known universe. He pissed off everyone he met at some point, and he met a whole lot of people. Only ever did one thing right in his whole sorry existence. Somehow, he raised a daughter with more brains than he ever had."

Zura bounded out of the booth. "Phyl? It's nice to see you again. You've had the *Beacon* upgraded since last I saw her."

A tall, muscular woman with close-cropped black and gray hair and a hawkish profile rose from her seat and clasped Zura's hand in greeting.

"I thought I taught you to keep a better eye on your surroundings, girl. I saw you come in, but you didn't see me. You're getting sloppy."

Zura shook her head. "Who says I didn't see you? I recognized the smell of that engine degreaser you drink from halfway across the room. You also taught me it's better to let people come to you in their own time. Once I saw you, I knew you'd make your presence known eventually."

Phyl snorted with laughter. "It's nice to know you were paying attention. Now, don't you be knocking my drink of choice. Torskian Ale is good stuff. It'll cure all your ails."

"Or kill enough brain cells you forget what those ails might be." Zura turned to Kit. "Kit, this is Captain Phylomena Harrington. Phyl, this is my...uh. Kit."

"Kit Armas. I'm the *Sun Sprite's* Security Officer," Kit explained as he rose to his feet and greeted Phyl.

"You taking on crew again? I thought you were done letting men on your ship?" Phyl's brow furrowed. "Armas. Why do I know that—son of a bitch, You're one of those cyborgs from the Drift. The Nono Club—no, that's not it—Nova Club, that's your place, right? What the hell are you doing running around the cosmos with *him*, girl? The Nova Club crew are supposed to be a little crazy even by Drift standards."

Kit crossed his arms over his chest and glowered. "We may be crazy, but we protect our own. Zura is under my protection, and I'm here to see she is safe."

Phyl's brows raised in surprise. "Uh huh. I'm going to need another drink before we get into the details of why you need protection. I know you've been on the straight and narrow since your dad died, so I'm going to assume that your current problem is related to your past life."

"It's Vin," Zura stated. If anyone knew why the hell Vin was sniffing around, it was Phyl. The wily freighter captain had been transporting goods of every kind across the galaxy since before Zura was born. Phyl always knew what was going on with friends and competitors alike, and Zura had long since learned not to ask where she got her information from.

Phyl snorted and gestured for them to join her. "Vin, huh? I should have guessed."

They moved tables before speaking further. Kit sat with his back against the wall while the two women sat beside each other.

"Vin tracked me down again and doesn't seem to be getting the hint I'm not coming back," Zura explained.

Phyl steepled her fingers in front of her and sighed. "That boy is six kinds of bad news. The smartest thing you ever did was to throw him off your ship."

Zura scoffed. "I should never have let the bastard on the *Sun Sprite* in the first place."

Phyl nodded and glanced over at Kit. "At least this one's better looking. Is he any smarter?"

Kit's face folded into a thunderous frown, and Zura had to stifle a laugh at his stormy expression.

"I'm a cybernetically enhanced soldier who survived more than ten years of combat duty. Please do not compare me to that pathetic creature who has been threatening Zura."

"I like him already. It's a pity I don't get too many runs that take me out to the Drift. I'm only here as a favor to a friend. His ship needed a part that this floating junkyard didn't carry, so I brought it out for him." Phyl turned to give Zura an intent look. "I heard a rumor you were operating out this way. Something about saving hundreds of lives and becoming a hero. Your daddy would be proud of you."

Zura shrugged. "It wasn't that big a deal. If you had been there, you'd have done the same thing."

"I'm really not much for heroics and near death experiences. I'm getting too old for that sort of nonsense."

"You're not that old, Phyl. I'm sorry it got so much publicity, though. I'm no hero, and if the news networks hadn't gotten wind of it, then Vin wouldn't know where I am. Do you think he's after the bonus money I got? He's always been a greedy bastard."

Phyl was quiet for a long moment, then leaned in closer to Zura. "This might not be about you.

Well, not entirely. I think this might concern your father."

"Dad? Why? He's been dead almost a year now, and I walked away from our old life. Why would Vin care about him, or me for that matter? He never showed this much interest in me when I was with him."

"Russ Watson was many things, most of them aggravating, but he wasn't completely selfish. He told me once that he was trying to make sure you and your brother had a shot at a better life if you wanted it. Did he ever tell you about his insurance policy?"

Zura nearly choked on her drink. "Not you, too. Vin asked me about that. There's no insurance policy. Trust me, I checked. When dad died, he left me the *Sun Sprite*, his contracts, and a mountain of debt the size of Mons Olympus. That's it."

Phyl's gaze dropped to the ring Zura wore around her neck. "That's not all he left you. Somewhere in all his personal possessions and papers, you never saw anything that might give you a clue?"

"There was nothing else, Phyl. As for Dad's lucky ring, this thing isn't worth more than a few dollars." She caught the chain with her fingers, pulling out the worn, battered ring to look at it again. "It was never very lucky, either. If it were, he would still be alive."

Kit frowned and eyed the ring. "Didn't you tell me he always said that luck was a poor man's only insurance?"

"He did. It was one of his favorite expressions. Well, one of the ones I can repeat in polite company, anyway."

Phyl snorted with laughter. "Sounds about right." She took a drink from her glass and stared at it for a second before setting it down and looking hard at Zura. "Whatever failings that man had, he loved you and wanted you to have a good life. You know he and I weren't much for talking, but he told me in confidence one time that he was setting up something for you, an insurance policy to give you a way out. Whatever it was, he must have died before he got it finished or he would have told you what he was up to. Trust that idiot to get himself killed before he could do a good thing for once in his life."

"I don't understand, why are you only telling me about this now?" Zura demanded.

"I came looking for you a few months after your Dad died and found out you were already gone. I figured that whatever your dad had been planning, he'd told you about it and that's how you managed to walk away. Not many do that, you know. Most of us who try to leave the life don't make it very far."

"I was too stubborn to fail."

"Another trait you got from your daddy," Phyl said.

"It's so strange that he never said anything to me. He must have said something to Vin though." Zura was musing aloud, trying to organize her whirling thoughts.

"Or Vin overheard something he shouldn't have. That one was always lurking around, listening to other people's conversations, looking for any information he could use to his advantage," Phyl said.

Zura kept idly toying with her dad's ring as she worked through all she knew. "That would explain why he's still looking for me. He thinks I've got money. Joke is on him, I'm as broke as the day I left. I'm nearly clear of dad's debts, at least, but that's it.

"But you're doing okay. You found a way out, even without your daddy's help. I'm proud of you. Hell, maybe I'm getting soft in my old age, but I like knowing you're out there and doing well for yourself."

"Then take the block off your ship's communication so I can talk to you sometimes. In fact, while I'm making requests, I'd like it if you got your ass over to the Drift one day soon. I can put in a good word for you and maybe find you some work that doesn't require breaking more than one or two rules and regulations."

Phyl arched a brow. "The block's been gone since your daddy died. You just never tried to call me. As for the offer, I'm too old to go legit now."

"Not completely legit, just…less criminal." Zura grinned back at Phyl. The truth was she hoped she could offer Phyl a way out of her old life and into one with less risk. It would take some convincing, but she had to try.

"I'll consider it. Might be nice to change the scenery for a while. Places like this lost their charm a long time ago."

"You'd be welcome at the Nova. Any friend of Zura's is a friend of ours," Kit said.

Phyl flashed a wide grin, "I might take you up on that offer, Kit. I've seen the pretty boys you have fight at your club. It might be worth a return visit. I really do like this one, Zura. I can see why you let him on your ship."

Zura smiled to herself. Phyl didn't give out praise lightly, especially when it came to males of any species. It was nice to know she approved of Kit.

Kit grinned back. "I meant what I said before. You're welcome at the Nova anytime, but please don't call my fighters pretty."

Further conversation was halted by the arrival of a group of miners, including two Torskis so large their table shook as they ambled past. The big, burly aliens were both over seven feet tall and weighed at least four hundred pounds each. They claimed seats within earshot of Phyl's table, making it unwise to keep talking.

When the meal was over, they said their goodbyes and headed back to the *Sun Sprite*. At least she had gotten Phyl's word that she would be in touch. There was a time when Phyl had been like a mother to Zura. The older woman's on-again-off-again relationship with Zura's father had been too volatile to ever last, but Phyl was one of the few people Zura trusted completely.

They were nearly back to the ship when Kit finally spoke. "She's an interesting woman. I take it you were close once?"

"She hated my dad almost as much as she loved him. They were too much alike to ever stay together long, but she always looked out for me."

"When we get on board, we need to go through everything your father left you and try to figure out what this insurance policy was. She seemed convinced he left behind *something* important."

"We can try, but I have no idea what the hell it could be. I've been over it all so many times already."

"You've been over it. I haven't. Maybe I'll see something you missed."

"Maybe." Zura couldn't imagine what her father could have left her that she didn't already know about. If anyone but Phyl had even suggested it, she would have laughed at them. Phyl believed there was something, though, and apparently so did Vin. If she wanted Vin off her back, she needed to figure this out, fast.

A new thought struck her as they reached the airlock they needed to pass through to get to her ship. "If I'm rich and didn't know it, I'm going to be seriously pissed off at my dad."

Kit laughed. "If that's the case, then maybe you can buy us a bigger bed for the *Sun Sprite*."

CHAPTER NINE

Luke stood at the portal and watched as the *Sun Sprite* docked. He should be back at the club serving drinks and waiting for his brother and Zura to come to him. That would have been the smart choice. It was the option that didn't make him look like a smitten fool who couldn't wait to see his girl again. Of course, he could claim that it was Kit he was waiting to see, but that was only slightly less pathetic.

The truth was that he'd missed both of them more than he'd expected to. Oh, they had been in contact daily, but it wasn't the same thing as having his brother at his side or having Zura sandwiched between them while they slept. Being out of contact with Kit had affected him in ways he hadn't expected either. On some level, he had always been aware of his twin's presence, even if it was only the subconscious registration of Kit's bio-signs. Without even that faint reminder of his brother, Luke had felt completely alone. It gave him a deeper understanding of what Cyn must have gone through when she had lost her twin.

In the early years, the constant chatter from their batch siblings, other cyborgs, and command channels had been enough to make them all a little mad. Then they'd gone into battle, and he'd had to listen as, one by one, his friends and surrogate family had been injured or died. He didn't have to rely on his recordings of those terrible moments to remember them. He relived them in his nightmares.

Since Kit left, the nightmares had returned. Not as bad as they'd once been, but being alone had triggered thoughts of Luke's greatest fear, having to be alone, without Kit, or Cyn, or anyone he loved. By the time he'd sensed the return of Kit's bio-signs, he'd realized there was someone else he didn't want to live without. Zura. Just the thought of having her back in his arms soothed him in a way nothing else ever could.

Kit appeared through the door first and broke into a grin as soon as he spotted Luke. "It's good to be home again. Hell, I even missed your annoying presence."

"I missed you too. Mostly because with you gone I had more work to do. I swear half the quadrant heard you were away and decided that meant it was a free-for-all at the bar."

Kit frowned. "My club better be in one piece."

"*Our* club is fine. The customers who were dumb enough to cause trouble are all in medical or already off the station."

"Which one of our people put someone in medical? We should probably give them a raise."

Luke grinned. "Cyn and Owen. Those two are terrifying when they team up. The idiot who was hassling Teenie the other night came back, and he brought friends. Cyn spotted him on the security feed and came down to deal with it herself. We might need to consider letting her out of her office more often; she's mean when she's stuck doing paperwork too many days in a row."

Kit nodded. "Frankly, I'm thinking we might want to see if she wants a shot at the cage fights. Let her burn off some of that aggression in the ring."

"Brilliant idea. They'd love to see her kicking ass. Hell, so would I. So long as I wasn't the poor sap in the ring with her."

"If she says yes, I'm putting all my money on Cyn," Zura said as she joined them.

Luke had her in his arms a heartbeat later, his mouth slanting over hers as he kissed her before uttering a single word of welcome. She rose up on her toes and kissed him back, her arms twining around his neck as she opened her lips and let their tongues dance. Her curvy body pressed up hard against his, and his cock surged to full attention in seconds. He needed to be alone with her soon. He wanted to strip her naked and reclaim every inch of her soft skin and remind her that she belonged to him as well as Kit.

"We weren't gone that long," Kit finally muttered.

"Time is relative. You two were together, and I was here alone." Luke tore his lips from Zura's to answer Kit.

"I missed you, too," Zura said, her voice barely more than a silken whisper. "Universe help me, but I really did."

"You have no idea how happy I am to hear you say that. If you want to make me even happier, tell me that you have nothing pressing to do for the next few hours."

She grinned at him. "I'm all yours as soon as I oversee the offloading of my cargo. There isn't much, just some odds and ends I traded for with some of the miners. No more than ten minutes, I swear."

Luke groaned and sunk his fingers into her long hair, tugging her head back so he was looking into her eyes. "That's too long. Can't Kit do it?"

"I'm still on the ship's roster as crew. I can sign for it," Kit said, and Luke said a silent thank you to his brother for stepping up.

"Give me one good reason why I should leave before the job is finished. This is my livelihood we're talking about, after all."

"If you don't go with me right now, I'm going to take you back on board, strip you naked, and take you up against the nearest flat surface."

She laughed. "That sounds like a good reason for me to stay right here."

"Teasing a cyborg is a dangerous thing, gorgeous."

"Who said I was teasing?"

"Zura…" he groaned her name, and she laughed before kissing him again.

"Okay, okay. Kit, you're in charge. If you need me—"

"He'll figure it out. You're going to be out of contact for a while. Thanks. I owe you one."

Kit chuckled. "Take good care of our girl. I'll see you both at the bar tonight. We still have things to discuss."

Luke nodded and lifted Zura into his arms before turning on his heel and heading for the other side of the station. The ship was closer, but he wanted to put a locked door between them and everyone else on the station, including Kit. He needed time alone with Zura, and there was only one place in the Drift where he knew that could happen: his quarters. No one would bother them there.

"Dammit, Luke, put me down."

"No."

Zura swung her leg, catching him in the side with the heel of her boot. "Yes! If you carry me across the station like this, you're going to cause all sorts of gossip. I'm perfectly capable of walking."

"Do you really care what people think? What are they going to say that isn't true? I've missed you, and I want to take you to bed as soon as possible. That's true enough."

"They might think that one of the station's most eligible bachelors has finally fallen for a—never mind. Forget I said that."

He grinned at her. "That might also be true."

Her eyes widened. "Oh, really?"

"I'm not confirming or denying the possibility just yet. First, I need you naked. Then we'll talk."

Laughter and desire flared in her eyes, and she wrapped her arms around his neck. "In that case, I suggest you move your ass."

They made it to his quarters in record time, and Zura still couldn't believe he had actually broken into a run along the way. She should be embarrassed at the display they put on, but she wasn't. He did it because he wanted her and didn't care who knew it. It was the sexiest thing any man had ever done for her, and she was enjoying herself too much to worry what other people might think.

The best part was when they'd arrived at the doors to the Nova. The security guard on duty saw them coming and opened the door with a smirk, letting Luke in so he didn't even have to slow down. Cyn waved at them from behind the bar, then they were through the private doors and headed for the elevator to Luke's quarters.

She hadn't been to his rooms yet, and she was curious to see what it looked like. The moment they were inside, she burst out laughing. "You made your place look like this on purpose?" she asked as she took in the décor.

His living space looked like a small-scale replica of the bar itself, right down to the all-blue furnishings.

Luke shrugged slightly as he carried her through the living area toward what she assumed was the bedroom. The layout of Luke's space was a little different than Kit's but not by much. "We order furniture in bulk, so I went with what was available. It's comfortable enough. The bed was a special order, though."

"Of course it was." Zura glanced through the door, expecting to see a black or blue monstrosity, possibly with a mirror on the ceiling. Instead, the bed looked like it could be an antique. It had four posts that rose from the corners of the frame, and she would almost swear that both the posts and headboard were made of real wood. Not something that was easy to come by this far from a planet.

"Is that wood? Like, actual wood from a tree?" she asked as he carried her across the room and set her down in the middle of the bed.

"It is. Are we really going to talk about this right now?" Luke stripped his vest over his head, baring his muscular chest.

"We could, but now that you have my attention, I think I'd rather watch you undress. Keep going, please."

He did as she asked with a grin, tearing at the clasp of his pants and tugging them off without ever taking his eyes off her. The sight made her clench her thighs together as a flood of liquid heat soaked her panties. They might have been built to be soldiers, but her guys were both incredibly sexy, too. Watching them get naked never failed to kick her libido into overdrive.

"I missed you," she told him as she started pulling off her clothes.

"Even though Kit was with you?" he asked.

"You're not interchangeable. You know that, don't you? I'm fond of you both, but I like it best when all three of us are together. When we're apart, it's not the same." Her explanation surprised her because she hadn't consciously thought about it, but she knew it was the truth all the same. Her guys might be identical in many ways, but that didn't mean they were the same person. She cared about both of them equally, but differently. In fact, she was falling hard for them both.

"I'm glad you feel that way, gorgeous. I like it when we're all together, too. Though right now, I'm damned glad to have you all to myself."

She crooked her finger at him. "Now who is doing all the talking? Come here, lover, and I'll show you how much I've missed you."

He prowled over to her slowly, giving her time to admire the hard lines of his body and the thick erection he was sporting. By the time they were close enough to touch, her clit was throbbing in time to her heartbeat, and she was trembling in anticipation of what was to come. His mouth claimed hers in a sizzling kiss that made her entire body hum.

"Next time you leave, I'm coming with you," he whispered as he pressed her back onto the bed, pinning her beneath him.

"But your job…" she started to protest, but he cut her off with a shake of his head.

"My job is not as important as you are."

"Damn, you and your brother have some really good lines."

He nipped her lower lip. "It's not a line, it's a fact."

"I'm in so much trouble," she murmured, barely aware that she had spoken her thoughts aloud.

"That makes three of us." Luke sealed her mouth with another kiss, ending any further conversation.

They kissed and stroked each other until the fire blazing inside her grew to an inferno. It didn't matter that she and Kit had been together only a few hours ago. This was Luke, and she needed him, too.

He broke their last kiss with a groan and lifted his head. "I need more than this."

"Whatever you need, take it," she replied.

"Thank you, I will." He grinned and started kissing his way down her body. She watched the way his muscles flexed and strained as he held himself over her. When he reached her stomach, he pressed a single kiss to her navel before leaving the bed and sinking to his knees on the floor. She didn't have time to do more than lift her head before his hands found her hips and he slid her body across the bed until her legs were dangling over the edge of the mattress and he was staring at her with a wicked grin that made her heart skip a beat.

"What are you doing?" she asked.

"Taking what I need," he said as he gently lifted her legs to his shoulders. Before she could move her legs back, he straightened up, raising her off the bed until only her head and shoulders still were on the mattress.

Her next retort didn't make it past her lips before he buried his face into her pussy and began devouring her. He lashed and licked at her clit in short, fast swipes that had her seeing stars within seconds. She squirmed, testing the limits of her position, and quickly accepted that there was nothing she could do but hang on for the ride. Her fingers tangled in the bed sheets as her senses were overwhelmed.

"Luke!" she cried out his name as the first tremors of an orgasm started. He let her ride the waves of pleasure to the brink of release, then slowed down, denying her the one thing her body craved.

He changed movements, sweeping his tongue along her inner folds in slow, languid strokes that deliberately avoided her clit. He held her in sway, dictating the pace and keeping total control of her body. Sensation built on sensation until all she could think about was what he was doing, and all she could feel was the touch of his mouth and tongue. Only when she was shaking with the need to come did he give her what she needed.

He slid a finger deep into her channel, then latched onto her clit, sucking hard as he flicked it with the tip of his tongue. She groaned, arching her back as pleasure slammed into her. She was so lost that she barely noticed when he withdrew his finger from her pussy to press the honey-slicked digit against the rosebud of her anus.

When she moaned again, he pressed deeper. "Someday soon, I'm going to take you here while Kit fucks your pussy. Both of us buried deep inside you at the same time. I can't wait."

His words triggered a flood of erotic images of the three of them together, and it sent Zura spiraling into orgasm. She came hard, bucking her hips against his lips as she imagined what it would be like to be locked together with both her lovers at once. She wanted that to happen soon.

She was still recovering from her orgasm when Luke rose to his feet. He gently eased her legs from his shoulders, hooking her knees over his forearms as he rubbed his cock against the slick folds of her pussy. "Ready?"

She grinned and nodded. "Very."

Luke stared at the beauty stretched out beneath him and marveled at how much had changed in such a short time. Day and night, she was always in his thoughts. All it took to make him hard was the sound of her voice or a single touch of her hand. She was under his skin in a way he had never experienced before.

He drove into her sweet body with a groan of pleasure, not stopping until he was buried to the hilt inside her. This was what he had been dreaming of since she had left. Being with her. Watching her enchanting silver eyes gleam with desire as she moaned his name. She might have been the one to go away, but right now, it felt like he was the one coming home. To her.

He pulled out of her almost completely, then plunged into her again. He'd always held back with other women, afraid of hurting them because of his size and strength. He had learned he didn't have to do that with Zura. She could take him at his wildest. In fact, she liked him that way. Luke closed his arms around her legs, holding her in place as he let himself go. She gripped the sheets beneath her and moaned as he began to power into her. Her inner walls gripped his cock, milking him with every thrust. The air filled with the sounds of sex. Flesh on flesh, soft gasps, and low groans as they both gave in to the pleasure coursing through them.

He started moving faster, his thrusts coming harder as the heat between them built until he felt like he was standing on the surface of a star. Soon they were racing each other to the finish line, instinct overtaking every semblance of control. He came hard, emptying himself into her with a ragged groan that tore the breath from his lungs. She arched and cried out a few seconds later, the look of ecstasy on her face mirroring his feelings exactly. He released her legs and lowered them to the bed before partially collapsing on top of her and kissing her hard.

"I missed this."

She laughed softly and stroked his hair out of his face. "I missed you."

He kissed her again, tenderly this time. "I'll make you a promise. Every time you come back, I'll greet you like this. Maybe that will help."

"I'm sure it will. When you come with me, Kit can be in charge of welcoming me home. I think that's a hell of a plan."

"Me, too." He kissed her one last time and then pushed himself off her. "Get comfortable, I'll be right back."

He went to the bathroom and grabbed a cleansing cloth for himself and another for Zura. By the time he washed up and returned, she was resting in the middle of his bed. Her hair was fanned out over the pillows, and she was smiling at him with a look of total trust and contentment. It was the first time any woman had looked at him like that, and it made him walk a little taller.

"What?" she asked as he walked over to her. "Why are you looking at me that way?"

"Because you're beautiful. Because you are here with me. Do I need any other reason?"

"I suppose not." She rose to take the cloth from him, but he shook his head and gestured for her to lie down again.

"Let me."

He cleaned her slowly, and when he was done, he tossed the cloth back to the bathroom and joined her on the bed. She curled up against him, her soft curves filling his arms.

"You didn't have to do that."

He pressed a kiss to the crown of her hair. "I wanted to. I like taking care of you, Zura. Not because you need me to, but because I enjoy it. I hope you let us take care of you for a long time."

"How long are we talking?" she asked, her voice soft.

His answer came from the heart. "I'm thinking forever might be just enough time."

"That sounds...very permanent. Are you sure?"

He winked at her. "I'm sure. Don't ask me how, but I am. You have a problem with that?"

She was quiet for a moment, and then she gifted him with another heart-stopping smile. "You're crazy. Has anyone ever told you that before?"

"Crazy. Yes, it's been mentioned a time or two before. It's part of my charm."

"What if you change your mind someday?" she asked, and for the first time since he had known her, Luke heard real doubt in her voice.

"About you? I don't see that happening. You're good for me. For Kit, too. He was smiling when he walked off your ship today. He's been better in every way since you've become part of our lives. You did that. I can see us having a future together. Maybe kids someday. A real family."

"I never thought about it. You can have kids?"

He nodded. "We can. One of the few things the corporations did right when they released us was to let us know that we could have children if we wanted to. The inhibitor injections they gave us can be reversed."

"A family," she murmured softly. "I never thought that would be an option for me."

"It could be. I know it's too soon to talk about kids and a family yet, but I wanted you to know that was an option if you wanted it," he said, then tucked her in beside him and kissed her softly. "Tell me what you learned from that friend of yours while you were gone,"

"You heard it all, already."

"Tell me again. Maybe talking it through with me will give us another hint what this insurance policy might be."

Zura nestled in Luke's arms and told him everything Phyl had told her about her father, and her theories about what he could have left her. When she was done, she realized she had been playing with her dad's lucky ring as she spoke.

"I still don't have a clue what this insurance policy could be. Kit thinks it has something to do with this ring, but I don't see how. There's not even an inscription on it. It's just a black stone and a gold band."

Luke plucked it out of her grasp. "Have you ever had it appraised? Maybe the stone's worth something."

"I doubt it. If it were worth anything, Dad would have used it as betting collateral and lost it years ago."

"Do you mind if I take a closer look at it?" he asked.

"Go ahead." Zura reached up and undid the clasp on the necklace.

Luke sat up and looked at the ring for a minute, frowned, and muttered, "That's interesting."

"What? Did I miss something?" Zura asked as she tried to read the expression on Luke's face.

"I think this is a data crystal. I haven't seen one quite like this before, though. Hell, I haven't seen many of them at all. There aren't a lot around anymore."

"Data crystals are ancient tech. No one uses them."

"Exactly. By any chance is this ring a family heirloom?"

Zura nodded. "It's been in the family for generations."

Luke handed it back to her. "If that's what it is, maybe this fabled insurance policy of your father's is stored on it. I don't think we've got anything in the club that could read it. Could there be something on the *Sun Sprite*?"

Zura slipped the necklace back on as she thought about Luke's question. She had many of the *Sun Sprite*'s systems upgraded with the bonus money she'd gotten for her run through the storm with the vaccine, but not everything had been replaced. "I'm not sure."

He sighed. "We're going to have to get out of bed and go find out, aren't we?"

"I'm afraid so. I need to know if you're right and if there's anything stored on this relic." She tapped the ring.

Luke left the bed and shot her a disgruntled look. "Of course I'm right. I'm the smart twin."

She laughed and got out of bed to hunt down her clothes. "How could I have forgotten?"

"I don't know. You weren't gone that long. Don't worry; now that you're back I'll be sure to remind you and my brother. After all, Kit was with you all this time and he didn't figure it out. That clearly shows which one of us has the brains."

"How did you know what it was, anyway?" she asked.

He grinned at her. "You'd be amazed at the strange things I've been offered to pay off a bar tab at the end of the night. Old tech. Star maps. Weird pets from other planets. You name it, someone has probably tried to give it to me instead of paying me in a currency I can actually use. I've learned all sorts of things working behind that bar."

"I'm glad you did. Otherwise, I might never have known what this was. Dad should have told me the damned thing was a data storage device. It would have saved me a lot of grief."

"He probably thought he had more time. We all think that until suddenly our time is up and we're left with things we wanted to say and no more time to say them."

Zura finished dressing and joined Luke by the door. "Regrets?"

He took her hand in his and looked down at her, his dark eyes solemn. "Some, yeah. I've lost a lot of people I cared about in my life. There were things I wish I had told some of them, and a few things I wish I could take back. Those are mistakes I don't intend to make again. When it comes to you, Zura, I don't want to have any regrets.""

Her cheeks heated as he stared at her. "Me, either."

For one long moment, he watched her in silence, then nodded once and leaned down to kiss her. "Time to go see what's on that crystal. I'll contact Kit on the way and let him know what's going on."

"Tell him to meet us in the cockpit of the ship. I have a feeling that's where we'll find what we're looking for." Zura headed back to the *Sun Sprite*, one hand in Luke's and the other wrapped around her father's lucky ring. If there was something else her father had left her, she wanted to know what it was, and why he had hidden it away.

CHAPTER TEN

Kit was waiting in the small cockpit when the other two arrived. He moved out of the way to let Zura pass, noting the grim set of her lips as she slid past him without a word. She dropped into the pilot's seat and started looking over the controls, clearly looking for something. While she focused on the console, Kit looked at his brother.

Luke leaned in close and spoke in lowered tones to avoid disturbing Zura. "She's okay. Just determined to figure out what's on that crystal."

"Understandable. Did anyone come looking for her while we were gone?"

Luke shook his head. "No one."

A half-second later, Luke switched to their internal comm channel. *"Our friends were in touch, though. They've tracked down the vessel Ganzer and his two friends came in on. It's still in the Drift."*

"Fraxx. They never left?"

"Doesn't look that way. They're keeping an eye on them for us. If we need them, they're ready to step in." While all the surviving cyborgs had been freed, not all of them had chosen to leave corporate employment. There were enough cyborgs working as Drift security and enforcement officers to ensure that he and Kit could always call in a favor when they needed it. In return, they offered their fellow cyborgs cheap booze and permanent VIP status at the Nova.

"Found you!" Zura crowed in triumph.

Kit turned his head to find her on her knees, facing the wall beside the console she was examining.

"What did you find?" Luke asked.

She turned around, looking pleased with herself. "If I'm right, I found an old data crystal reader. If I'm wrong, I found a totally useless gizmo that serves no discernable purpose, which is what I thought it was the last time I noticed it. I was going to have it taken out when I could afford another round of upgrades. Good thing I didn't get around to that, yet."

"A very good thing. This way we don't need to wait to see what's on it, if anything," Kit agreed.

She undid the chain from around her throat and slid the ring into her hand before turning to face the wall again. "Here goes nothing."

They waited in silence while she fiddled with the ring and the reader, cursing under her breath as she tried to work with the unfamiliar technology.

Finally, there was a pause, then a yelp of surprise. "*Re'veth*! That son of a bitch."

"What?" Luke asked, crowding in closer.

"Remember when I said that if he had left me a bunch of money I was going to be pissed?" she asked.

"I do," Luke said.

"Well, I'm pissed. In fact, I'm about three levels past that. I could have paid off every outstanding debt he left me if I'd known about this. Why didn't he tell me?" Her voice raw with emotion barely kept in check, she slapped her hand against the wall in frustration.

Kit hated that she was hurting. He knew she was feeling the grief of her father's passing all over again, and there was nothing he could do to help except be there for her. "He must have had his reasons for keeping it a secret. Is there anything else, or is it just a cash windfall?"

She squared her shoulders and lifted her head to look at the screen again before answering. "There's something here with my name on it, too. One second, I'm going to save this to the main system. I'd rather read the rest in comfort instead of sitting on the floor."

A few seconds later she was rising to her feet. The moment she was standing, Kit reached for her hand and drew her into his arms. He didn't say anything, he simply held her until he felt some of the tension leave her body.

"Thanks, I needed that."

She raised her head to smile at him, and he did his best to ignore the tears that gleamed on her lashes and dampened her cheeks.

"You don't have to thank us for taking care of you. It's our privilege to do it," Luke reminded her, his hand stroking down her back.

"I'm not used to having anyone around to take care of me. Even before Dad died, he wasn't that kind of father."

"Yet, he saved up all that money for you," Kit pointed out.

"Or stole it. God only knows where he got his hands on that kind of cash. We lived from job to job. I don't understand any of this."

"When you're ready, I think you should read the file with your name on it. Maybe there are some answers in it."

Zura nodded slowly. "I'm ready now. Let's head to the galley. That way we can all be comfortable. I mean, if you two want to stay. If you need to head back to the club, I understand."

"I let Cyn know what was going on while you two were heading back here. She's not expecting either of us back tonight. We're not going anywhere," Kit said.

"Thank you. I…just…thank you." She hugged him hard before releasing him and doing the same to Luke.

"Like Kit said, we're here for you. Always," Luke said, looking over Zura's head at Kit.

Always. Kit heard the word his brother spoke, and it struck a chord deep in his heart. That's what he wanted with Zura: always and forever. He knew it would soon be time to tell Zura what they wanted and find out if that's what she wanted, too. If she didn't, he was swearing off women and love for the rest of his damned life. Andrea had been a mistake, he knew that now. Zura though…if she didn't want forever with them, it was going to destroy him, and he knew it.

Zura led the way to the galley, which was the closest place with a decent sized monitor and seating for all of them. She was grateful that neither man mentioned her tears. They were there for her, offering her their support while never making her feel weak or foolish for her momentary lapse.

When her father died, she had been so busy trying to deal with everything that she never took the time to stop and grieve properly. She had taken all her feelings and stuffed them into a quiet corner of her heart. Discovering that he had left something for her, even if he died before he could tell her what he was planning, brought back all the grief and anger she had never really dealt with. As much as she wanted to know what was on the file with her name, she wasn't looking forward to the pain that would come with it.

When she took a seat, Kit claimed the chair to her left and Luke the chair to her right. Each of them took one of her hands in theirs, another silent offer of support that touched her deeply.

"Let's get this over with," she said and took a slow breath before uttering her next command. "Computer, display file Zura One."

Instead of the document she was expecting, a video recording of her dad appeared on the galley's main screen, and her heart broke all over again.

"Daddy?" She hadn't meant to speak out loud, but her shock at seeing his face again was too much. His hair was longer, and there was a lot less gray in it than the last time she had seen him. She would look at the date on the file later to be certain, but she guessed the recording was at least ten years old.

"Hey, Zee. It's me. If you're watching this, then I'm dead, and you're on your own. I'm sorry about that, baby. I was hoping to see you grow up and find your place in the world before I kicked it, but hey, shit happens."

He fidgeted in his chair for a second before continuing. "The day you were born, I started putting aside a bit of money from every job I did. It wasn't much, but it started to add up as the years passed. I wanted you to have choices. Maybe do better than I did. I wanted that for both you and your brother. I wasn't much of a father. I know that. You and Royan, you were better than I deserved."

He scrubbed a hand over his stubble-covered chin and sighed. "*Fraxx*, I'm no good with this mushy crap, and I'm even worse at talking about shit like my own mortality. When you're older, I'll tell you all of this myself. For now, I just wanted you to know that I'm proud of you, and I—I love you. Take good care of my ship, and watch your back, baby. If there's life after this shit show, you know I'll be watching over you."

The recording ended suddenly, leaving her staring at a blank screen. Her heart ached, and her thoughts were so tangled she didn't know where to start. Why hadn't he ever told her about the money? Or the ring for that matter?

Luke squeezed her hand. "You look like him."

"Apart from all the blue, you mean." She gestured to her face and hair.

"I happen to like all the blue. It's my favorite color, remember?" Kit said, kissing her cheek.

"I remember." Zura nodded. "At least now I know what Vin's after, and what the insurance policy really is. I can't believe he never told me anything about it. I never expected a video, or for him to say what he said. I never thought I'd hear his voice or see him again. He looked so young there. I couldn't have been more than sixteen or so when he made that."

"Do I need to get us all drink now?" Kit asked.

"Hell yes, I'm going to need a drink. Probably several."

Luke nodded. "Drinks all around. First, though, I think you should arrange for that money to be transferred somewhere safe."

"Good thinking. I need to tell Royan, too. He's going to lose his mind when he finds out. His share will put him a lot closer to being able to put a down payment on a ship of his own."

"You're giving him half?" Luke asked.

"Of course I am. He's my brother. We might not be as close as you Armas siblings, but he's the only family I've got."

"He left you to run the *Sun Sprite* alone. What kind of family does that?" Kit muttered.

"If I asked him to, he'd be there for me in a heartbeat." Zura snapped her fingers. "In case you two have forgotten, I'm not much for asking for help."

"You have a point," Luke said with a chuckle.

"I'm glad you asked us for help, little one."

She turned to Kit and laughed. "I don't recall asking for anything. You overheard my conversation with Ganzer and sent him packing, and then Luke ran off those two jerks Vin sent. After that, I was somehow stuck with the two of you."

"Are you complaining?" he asked, leaning in until they were nose to nose.

"Never. You two are the best thing to ever happen to me." She closed the last inch between them and kissed him.

"We feel the same way about you," Luke said, lifting their joined hands to kiss her fingers as she kissed his brother. Kit's teeth grazed her lower lip, his mouth slanting across hers.

One kiss led to another, then another. It was easier to lose herself in passion than to face the questions and grief that waited for her once this moment was over. Knowing that they would be there for her no matter what came next, made her feel like the luckiest woman in the galaxy.

They had become friends, then lovers, and now she couldn't imagine a future without both Kit and Luke in it.

She didn't know how it would work yet, but she was going to try and keep them both.

Forever.

CHAPTER ELEVEN

The peace didn't last for long. Vin started sending messages to her two days after she and Kit got home. She had long since blocked him from being able to contact the *Sun Sprite* to prevent her from having to see his pleas for forgiveness and for her to return. Apparently, someone had tipped him off to the fact she was staying at the Nova, though, because he was now sending messages to her via the club.

She had only looked at the first one, and once she confirmed he had nothing new to say, she had deleted it, and asked Kit and Luke to delete any new messages that arrived. These days she had much better things to do with her time than worry about Vin. He was her past, and for the first time in her life, Zura felt like she had a shot at a truly happy future. She refused to let Vin take that away from her. He had stolen enough from her already.

As the days passed, things between Kit, Luke, and herself only got better. She stayed at the club every night. She kept her own room, though she really only used it to store her belongings. She spent every night wrapped up in her lovers' arms, and every morning she woke up feeling more certain that this was where she belonged. With them.

The only thing stopping her from embracing her new life were the emotional aftershocks that hit after seeing the video from her father. He should have told her about the money. He likely thought he was protecting her, and it was all a misguided attempt at being a good father. Instead, he died and she was left with one more thing to be angry at him about. What if she had never figured out what the ring was? What if she had spent the rest of her life struggling because he loved his secrets almost as much as he loved his vices?

He had been dead for the better part of a year. She thought she was past the sudden onset of tears or strange flashes of anger over his death, but ever since she had played his message, there were moments where her grief was as fresh and raw as the day he died. The only difference was that this time, she had Luke and Kit in her life. They were never far away, helping her however they could. They were her anchors, and she was grateful for them both.

It was deep into the night, and Zura lay between her men, her mind racing too fast for her sleep. A muffled chime from her comm device sounded, the tone indicating she had received a recorded video message. Happy to be distracted from her thoughts, she eased herself out from between her still sleeping men. Stifling a yawn, she pulled on one of their discarded shirts and went in search of her comm device.

Maybe the message was Royan finally getting back to her. She'd tried to contact him right away, but he hadn't answered her. So she'd left a message telling him she had good news, but nothing else. She wanted to see his face when she broke the news that she had found their father's infamous insurance policy, and what he had stashed away for them. So far, he hadn't called back, but that wasn't unusual. He could be working long hours, or more likely he was busy enjoying the company of a pretty girl or a long-running card game. He had inherited more than their father's looks; he also shared a few of their old man's vices.

The chime sounded again, and she padded across the room to retrieve the device from the drawer Luke had dropped it in after dinner. He had taken it from her and announced that they were all done working for the night. After that, her guys had carried her to bed and made love to her until they were all sated.

Comm device in hand, she left the bedroom and went to find a quiet place to watch her message, somewhere she wouldn't wake Kit and Luke. She ordered up a mug of cocoa first, and then she took a seat at the table and activated her device. Sure enough, she could see there was a newly recorded message from Royan's comm device.

The audio started before anything appeared on the screen, but she didn't need to see his face to recognize her brother's voice. "Hey, sis. It's me. Apparently, I'm in trouble, and this guy keeps saying it's all your fault."

The video feed kicked in, and Zura's heart twisted in her chest. Royan looked like he had been on the wrong side of a serious ass kicking. His brown hair was matted with what looked like blood, his lips were cracked and bleeding, one eye was swollen shut, and there were more bruises showing beneath the several days' worth of stubble on his cheeks.

"Damn it, Roy. What the hell happened to you?" she murmured to herself, her eyes locked on the screen.

"Hey, Zura. Since you wouldn't do this the easy way, I had to come up with a different way to get your attention. I bet you're listening to me now, huh?" The video swung around and she found herself staring at a face from her past. Vin Collins.

"Oh, *fraxx*," she groaned as he sneered and gave her a little wave.

"You should have met with me when I asked nicely. Now your little brother is caught up in your mess. Don't worry, though. He'll be fine as long as you do exactly what I tell you to. You may not like taking orders, but you better *fraxxing* follow these, or Royan will pay the price. Here's what's going to happen. In ten hours, you are going to be at the Torex mining station at the far end of the Drift. You will dock, disembark, and go directly to a bar called the Blast Zone. If you don't know where that is, then you better find out, fast. You and I are going to have a nice, cozy chat about a few things, and then you're going to hand over the *Sun Sprite* and everything else your old man left you when he died."

Vin turned the camera back on Royan again, but he kept talking. "That's the deal. When I find what I'm looking for, you and your brother can leave. Tell anyone else about this and Royan dies a nasty death. Don't tell anyone where you're going or what you're doing. No one else comes with you. No exceptions. I'll see you ten hours from the time I see this message was received. Once you dock, you'll get more instructions. Follow them. Your brother's life depends on it."

The recording ended, and the screen went blank.

Ten hours. He hadn't given her much time. The trouble with flying in and around the Drift was that you couldn't use FTL drive. The distances were really too short for Faster Than Light travel, and reentry to normal space was insanely dangerous with that many ships and other objects floating around. She would have to rely on her regular engines, and that meant it would take time to get to her destination.

At least the Blast Zone was a good place to meet. It was a well-known bar on one of the biggest ore processing stations in the Drift. It was a popular place for crews to kick back and relax after a long shift. There would be plenty of people there, and witnesses would make it more likely that Vin behaved himself.

Her mind started to race, and she took a deep breath, forcing herself to focus on facts. She needed a plan, and there was no time for guilt or recriminations. Not now. Royan was in trouble, and it was her fault. She had to get him back. Once she did that, she would deal with Vin. The son of a starbeast was going to pay for what he had done.

"Hang in there, Royan. I'm coming." She rose to her feet and headed to the bedroom to retrieve her clothes. She made it as far as the doorway and then froze as she spotted Luke and Kit fast asleep on the bed they all shared. She had been on her own so long that she hadn't even considered that she didn't have to do this alone. Hell, she would have a much better chance of pulling this off if she had help. All she had to do was ask, and they would come with her. She wasn't sure she could ask that of them, though. The club was their business, as well as their home. They needed to be here, taking care of things. Royan was her family, not theirs. He was her responsibility.

She grabbed her clothes and slipped out again, dressing in the main room to avoid making any noise that might wake them up. This wasn't their fight. If something happened to them while they were helping her, she would never forgive herself. Part of her was certain that she needed to do this on her own, but her heart hurt every time she thought about leaving them. She knew that if their roles were reversed, she would want to know what was going on and would offer to help any way she could.

She stood there in the dark for an uncertain eternity, but in the end, she knew she couldn't walk away without at least saying goodbye. Luke and Kit deserved better than waking up tomorrow morning to discover she had gone to face Vin without them. It wasn't her decision to make. It was theirs.

"Guys? Wake up. Something happened, and I think I'm going to need your help."

* * * *

Kit couldn't keep still. Every time he sat down, he was back on his feet again a few minutes later. He wanted to hit something. No, he wanted to hit someone. Specifically, Vin Collins.

He paced the length of the meeting room, ignoring the annoyed looks he was getting from the others. Cyn was present, and so were two of their friends who were employed at Corp-Sec, corporate security and enforcement for the Drift. Mack and Dash were both good men, and they weren't happy to hear that the peace of the Drift had been threatened.

They had spent the last forty minutes asking Zura what seemed to be an endless list of questions and helping to put together a plan. All six of them were in one of the club's private rooms, sitting around a table as they worked out the best way to proceed.

"You're sure you want to go through with the meeting? We could have him arrested at the Blast Zone and put an end to this," Dash asked, running his hand through his spiky blond hair.

"If you do that, Royan's dead. They'll hold him somewhere else to make sure I do what I'm told. I have to make the meeting, and I have to do it alone."

Luke snarled in frustration. "I really hate that part of the plan. You shouldn't be going anywhere without us."

"If he sees me with a pair of big, angry looking cyborgs, he's going to figure out something is up. He knows I'm staying here, guys. Even Vin isn't *that* stupid. I've already agreed to take you along, but you have to be smuggled onboard, and you must stay out of sight on the *Sun Sprite*. In fact, I'm counting on you two staying there and keeping tabs on my ship. I don't trust Vin not to send someone to try and break in while I'm at this meeting."

Kit rose to his feet and slammed his palm down on the table in front of him. "One of us is going with you, little one. There's no *fraxxing* way we're letting our future wife go to meet her enemy alone."

The entire room lapsed into silence, and everyone turned to stare at Kit. Well, everyone one but Cyn. She leaned back in her chair and started to laugh.

"Did you just call me your future wife?" Zura asked, looking utterly stunned.

"I did." It wasn't the romantic proposal he and Luke had been planning, but he wasn't going to back down now. She was the one he wanted. The one both of them wanted to spend the rest of their lives with, and there wasn't a snowball's chance in a supernova that she was going to get her brother back without them.

"You're both insane," she muttered.

"Yeah, we are. We're both crazy about you, gorgeous," Luke said, rising to his feet as well.

Cyn looked at her brothers and laughed harder. "Damn, I'm glad I'm here to witness this firsthand. I wouldn't have missed this for anything."

"Not helping, Cyn," Luke snapped.

"Now? You two want to do this now?" Zura asked incredulously.

"Yes, now. Given everything that's going on, now might be all we have." Kit reached down and took her hand, pulling her gently into his arms. For a moment, he thought she might resist, but in the end, she came to him willingly.

"You really do need to work on your timing."

"That's Vin's fault, not ours," Luke muttered, moving in behind her so that she was caught between them.

"Married, huh?" she whispered.

"Uh huh. It doesn't matter if you say yes to us now or later. Eventually, that's what we're going to be. Married," Kit told her.

Zura turned her head to look over her shoulder at Luke. "Is this what you want, too?"

"Absolutely. The master of romance and seduction here might have rushed things a little, but yeah, I'm sure. You are the one we want, Zura. Forever."

Her eyes were shining as she nodded. "Then, may the universe help me, my answer is yes—even though you two forgot to actually ask me, first."

Kit crushed her to him and kissed her hard. "Mine now."

Mack snickered from the other side of the table. "I would never have believed this if I wasn't seeing it with my own eyes."

"Seeing it? I'm recording this for posterity," Dash said, grinning from ear to ear as he touched a finger to the corner of his left eye.

"I'm going to want a copy of that video, Dash. Hey, you two. If you let go of your girl for a minute, I have something to say to Zura," Cyn said.

"Not yet. Kit, share the love, will you? She's going to be mine too," Luke grumbled.

Kit let go of Zura after one last kiss, releasing her so his brother could draw her into his arms next.

"Hello, gorgeous." Luke lifted her into his arms before kissing her, and Kit swore he had never seen his brother look so content. Zura completed them both and made them stronger than ever.

"If this is what love looks like, then I think I'll give it a miss," Mack commented.

"Oh, I don't know. I think love-struck and goofy is a good look for them."

"Will you two quit baiting my brothers? I want to welcome Zura into the family."

Kit stepped back as Luke released Zura, who turned and headed straight for Cyn. Their sister barely had time to get to her feet before Zura was hugging her.

Cyn looked stunned for a moment and then hugged her back. "I wanted to tell you that I was beginning to give up hope these two would ever find someone who could put up with their shit. I'm glad they have you in their lives. When you come home, we're going to throw the three of you one hell of a wedding."

"I am, too. I'm glad to have all of you in my life. What I have to do next would be a lot more daunting if I didn't have all of you in my corner."

"Speaking of which, you three need to get going," Mack said.

"Don't forget to use the encrypted channel for any communications with us. We'll be close by, monitoring everything, and there will be a team waiting for you when you land. We'll find your brother and take out Vin, along with anyone with him," Dash said.

"If he lives that long," Luke muttered under his breath.

Mack grunted. "As a representative of the corporations, I have to remind you that killing Vin Collins would be interfering in an active investigation."

"He plans on stealing from Zura, and he's kidnapped her brother. Do you really think we're going to let him live?" Luke demanded.

"No, I don't. I just had to point it out for the record. Good luck to all three of you. We'll see you when you return with your brother, Zura," Dash said.

After that, there was a quick round of goodbyes, and then Zura headed for her ship while he and Luke went with Mack to another hangar and slipped onto a Corp-Sec shuttle. They would rendezvous with the *Sun Sprite* once she was en route and away from watchful eyes. They'd stay linked just long enough for he and Luke to transfer over, and then the three of them would be on their way to the far side of the Drift.

The moment they were on board the *Sun Sprite*, Kit planned on making things between them official. Whatever happened next, they would face it together.

CHAPTER TWELVE

Zura was alone in the cockpit, prepping for departure as she tried to process everything that had happened in the past two hours. She was still a little stunned by it all, and once they were on their way, she had a few things she needed to say to them both.

The launch went smoothly, and shortly thereafter, she made the mid-flight connection with the Corp-Sec shuttle carrying Kit and Luke. Once they were onboard and they were on their way again, she activated the autopilot function and went in search of her men. She found them in the ship's recreation area. It had a treadmill and a few other bits of fitness equipment that had once belonged to her father or her brother or both. There was a large screen for watching entertainment videos and a couple of comfortable chairs.

It was the roomiest area on the ship, and she wasn't surprised to find them there. What did surprise her was what they were doing. They had dragged the chairs and fitness equipment up against the walls, and then filled the empty space with what looked to be every mattress and pillow on the ship. They must have raided all the guest quarters on board because the bed they were building was more than big enough to accommodate all three of them.

"What have you done to my ship?" she asked as she walked into the room.

"Temporary renovation," Luke replied as he dropped an armload of bedding onto one of the mattresses.

"There's no way we were all fitting into your bed, so we made a new one." Kit was on his knees a few feet from her, rummaging through a stack of pillows.

"You made a new one in the middle of my rec area?"

"I don't know if you've noticed, but your ship isn't exactly spacious, and her refit isn't scheduled until next month. It was here or the cargo bay, and after hearing the stories about all the strange things you've hauled over the years, I'm not sleeping in there until the whole thing is decontaminated," Luke said.

"Grab a seat, we'll be done here soon, little one."

"That is unless you want to help? The sooner we get this finished, the sooner we can test out the new bed." Luke grinned at her and waggled his brows.

"We can test it later. I need to talk to the two of you first." Zura walked around the makeshift bed and sank down into one of the chairs.

"Is something wrong? You look unhappy." Kit got up, walked over to where she was seated, and then crouched at her feet.

"What is it?" Luke said as he came over to join them.

"I'm not unhappy."

"You're not happy, either." Kit drew his finger gently down her furrowed brow.

"I'm…I just….I have to ask you something. Are you two sure you want to do something as crazy as get married? I mean really sure. I know what you said when we were with the others, but now that it's the three of us alone, you're allowed to say something if you aren't sure this is what you want. We're all wound up right now; I understand if you want to rethink things."

Kit swore under his breath, and Luke shook his head before speaking again. "I'm not *fraxxing* changing my mind. Now or ever."

Luke dropped to his knees beside his brother and took her hand in his. "We want you."

She turned to nuzzle his hand. "I just needed to hear you say it. If we do this, then it's going to be with no regrets and no doubts."

"The only regret I have is that it took me so long to see how amazing you are. When I think of the time we lost..." Kit murmured softly.

"We found each other when we were supposed to. You were there for me when I needed you most. That's all that matters," Zura said, every word coming straight from her heart.

Luke nodded. "Exactly. All that matters is that we found each other. Nothing else. We're going to be together, and no one is going to get in the way of that happening."

"You're perfect for us. I would also like to point out that you already said yes. There's no going back now. You're committed," Kit told her.

"Forever," Luke added before leaning in to kiss her gently.

Forever. It was the most incredible word she had ever heard. When the kiss ended, she pulled back enough so she could look into their eyes. "Then there's only one more thing to say. I love you. Both of you. It's crazy and reckless and maybe even foolish, but I do, and I am never going to stop."

"I love you too." Luke kissed her again, then moved back to give Kit his turn to speak.

"Zura Watson, you are amazing, beautiful, and more than I ever believed I deserved. You've made my life better. You've made *me* better. I love you," Kit said. He reached into his pocket and pulled out a simple ring made of three strands of braided metal. Two of the bands were silver, while the third one was a bright cobalt blue.

"Marry us?" Luke asked as Kit held out the ring.

Zura blinked back the tears that threatened to fall as she looked from Luke to Kit and back to the ring again. For once in her life, the stars were aligning and her dreams were being realized, even the ones she'd never dared to admit to. Passion was one thing, but true, lasting love with someone who could not only accept who she was, but embrace it, was something she never truly believed would happen. She'd been wrong, because it hadn't happened just once, but twice.

"Yes," she whispered, holding out her hand so that Kit could place the ring on her finger.

"The next time you step off this ship, you'll do it wearing our ring. Whatever comes next, we're going to face it as a trio, and everyone will know you belong to us."

She nodded, barely able to tear her eyes from her new ring. "We belong to each other. Always."

"Yes, we do." Kit murmured, kissing her fingers before letting go of her hand.

Luke was beaming from ear to ear. "Now that we've got that settled, I have a thought about what to do for the next few hours. The way I figure it, we're in the calm before the storm right now. I can't think of a better way to spend that time than making love to our new fiancée."

Desire quickened her pulse. "I think that sounds like a very good way to pass the time. Far better than sitting around, worrying about things I can't change."

"We're going to get your brother back, Zura. He's coming home, and Vin's going to pay for what he's done," Kit spoke the words like a vow.

"I know we are. I would have done this alone, but I'm glad I don't have to," she said.

"You're never going to be alone again," Luke whispered.

"I know." She held up the ring. "That's what this is, a promise that none of us will ever have to be alone."

Kit pulled her into his arms and rose to his feet, taking her with him. "I like the sound of that."

Luke stripped off his clothes so fast he tore his shirt, but he didn't care. He only had one thing on his mind, and that was making love to Zura. He craved the warmth of her touch and the sound of her voice. He wanted to sleep every night with her scent on their sheets and his arms wrapped around her soft body.

Leaving his clothes in a heap on the floor, he stepped onto their makeshift bed and dropped to his knees. He wrapped one hand around his cock as he watched Kit strip Zura with a singlemindedness that matched his own. The moment she was naked, Kit kissed her, then pushed her gently toward the bed. Luke held out his hands to her, and she took them, letting him draw her down onto the bed and into his arms.

She draped her arms around his neck, and he bowed his head to kiss her. Her lips were sweet, and as his tongue swept into her mouth, he tasted a hint of the glazed pastry she had eaten during the long meeting earlier. Luke had watched her devour every bite, and every time she licked her lips or taken another nibble, his dick had ached with longing. Even watching her eat was a turn-on.

Kit finished undressing and joined them, kneeling behind Zura and pressing a kiss to her bare shoulder before undoing the tie that held her hair back. It spilled down her back, and Luke speared his fingers into it, wrapping several strands around his hand. He tugged on her hair, guiding her head to one side until her throat was bared and Luke could see her pulse point jump with each heartbeat. He kissed his way to her ear and then down her neck.

"Mine," he said, the word rising from his throat on a low rumbling groan.

"Always," she whispered.

The two of them worked in concert, stroking and tasting every inch of her until she was trembling in their arms. Only then did Kit move backward, coaxing her into a seated position so that her back was pressed against his chest and her legs were stretched out in front of her. Luke slowly slid his hands from her ankles to her knees, encouraging her to draw her legs up. The moment she did so, Kit reached around and hooked his hands under her knees.

"Lean back, little one. I've got you."

Looking at her laid out like a feast before him, Luke had to fight to draw his next breath. She was so much more than he had ever imagined they'd have during the long, lonely nights he and Kit had spent as soldiers, fighting a war they had no stake in, against an enemy who was as trapped by fate and circumstances as they were.

"You take my breath away," he told her as he settled himself on the bed, his face between her thighs. He traced the swollen lips of her pussy with one finger as the heady scent of her arousal filled his senses. She was close to being ready for them, but he didn't want her ready. He wanted her out of her mind with need and wanting so that when they took her together, there would be no room for fear or worry. There would only be pleasure: hers and theirs.

He leaned in and ran his tongue over the same path his finger had just taken, and she moaned softly in response. He pushed in deeper, using his tongue and fingers to bring her to the point of orgasm without letting her go over the edge. He flicked the tip of his tongue across the swollen nub of her clit again and again, enjoying every sigh and moan that fell from her lips.

"Please. I want..." she gasped brokenly, not even completing her request.

Those were the words he was waiting to hear.

He quickened his pace, sliding his fingers deep into her channel as he lapped and sucked at her honey-sweet folds. Her breath came in soft pants, and within moments, she cried out in ecstasy as her orgasm hit. Luke could hear his brother whispering to Zura as she came, her entire body quaking with the force of her release. He lifted his head to watch her in her pleasure, drinking in the intoxicating sight of their mate lost to all but the sensations coursing through her.

Zura was still struggling to gather her scattered wits when Kit released her legs and pressed one last kiss to the side of her throat. He stretched out beside her, his big frame spanning the length of the bed. His hard cock rose up from between his thighs, and he tapped his chest with one finger while giving her a sultry grin.

"Come up here, little one. I need you."

She pushed herself up off the mattress and made her way to his side. Instead of straddling him, though, she leaned down and kissed him first. He buried his fingers in her hair and kissed her back, his tongue slipping into her mouth to dance with hers. She was still kissing Kit when Luke moved in behind her. His hands landed on her hips and without warning, he lifted her up, then settled her back down so that her knees landed on either side of Kit's waist.

"In a hurry, Luke?" she asked with a chuckle as she broke the kiss to look around from her new vantage point.

"Maybe."

"Subtle. Very subtle," Kit said as he reached up to cup her breasts in his hands.

"And you claim to be the romantic one in this relationship," she added, then yelped in protest when Luke swatted her ass hard enough to sting a little.

"You do that again, and I will find a way to hurt you," she warned, but there was a subtle burr to her voice that sounded almost like a…purr?

"Damn, do that again, Zura. That is seriously sexy," Luke said.

"I…I didn't know I could do that at all." *Kyrnning* was something that Pherans did when they were highly aroused. It was a sound she had never made before.

Kit gave her a look of pure male satisfaction. "We just made you *kyrnn*, didn't we?" he asked before rising up to seal her mouth with a long, torrid kiss.

He drew her down until she was lying on him, mouths mated, tongues entwined, his cock pressing along the seam of her pussy. All it took to bring the thick head of his cock flush against her entrance was a shift of her hips. Kit groaned as they came into such intimate contact, the low sound rolling through her like the tolling of a bell. He raised his hips and slid himself home an inch at a time. He went slowly, drawing out the moment their bodies became one. Lying skin to skin with Kit, she could feel his heart pound in time with hers. She let herself get lost in the moment, letting everything else fall away.

Luke stroked his hand down her spine as he moved in behind her. There was a soft snick of a cap opening, and then his fingers slipped between her nether cheeks. He moved slowly, his fingers slick with something that felt cool and tingled slightly where it touched her skin. Before she could ask what it was, Luke spoke.

"It's just gel with a little numbing agent in it. I don't want this to hurt, and it's your first time," he said.

"We're going to take this slow, little one," Kit told her between kisses.

"Not too slow, I hope."

Both men chuckled, but it was Kit who spoke first. "I think we all want this too much to move *that* slowly."

He arched his hips, pushing himself another half inch inside her, then withdrawing again. His slow, shallow thrusts were too light to do anything but tease, and soon she was rocking over him, trying to take more than he was giving her. Behind her, Luke continued his slow exploration, working a finger into her tight rosebud, penetrating her with the same slow rhythm as Kit. When he added another finger, Zura tensed, then relaxed again as the faint burn faded away, leaving only pleasure behind.

"Okay?" Luke murmured, bending over her to press a trail of kisses across her back.

"Don't stop," she said, pushing back against his hand for the first time.

"You ready for more, gorgeous?"

Zura didn't hesitate. "I'm ready."

Kit stroked her cheek, bringing her focus back to him. "I love you."

His next kiss was tender, slow, and sensual, capturing her senses and filling her with liquid heat. Luke withdrew his fingers from her body, but before she could adjust to that loss, she felt a new, thicker pressure as he moved in tight behind her.

She exhaled and pushed back, allowing him to enter her. There was a brief sting of pain, and then she was caught up in a maelstrom of pleasure so intense she forgot to breathe until her lungs were burning. She gasped, drawing in a deep lungful of air and then releasing it again in a rush as Luke pushed deeper inside her. Neither man moved a muscle, giving her time to adjust. When she was ready, she took the initiative, rocking back, then forth between them as another soft purr rose from her throat.

"Oh yeah, just like that," Luke groaned, moving with her now.

"Ours, now," Kit said as he joined their dance.

The three of them moved as one, and soon, Zura couldn't tell where she ended and they began. Hands stroked, lips touched, bodies blended together so completely that she was certain even their hearts beat as one. Pleasure built on pleasure until she was trembling on the brink of orgasm, the sounds her lovers were making telling her that they weren't far behind. At the moment her release hit, she cried out and came. Overwhelmed by everything she was feeling, her world faded to gray, and she let herself drift, knowing her men would keep her safe.

Kit held Zura gently as her eyes fluttered closed, and she slumped against his chest. The subtle scent of her perfume grew stronger, and he slowly realized that she had marked them both with her scent. They weren't simply engaged anymore. Her Pheran side had claimed them as her *vardo*, her life mates.

He came harder than he had ever done before, the power of his orgasm tearing a groan from his lips as he emptied himself inside her. Luke's low groan heralded his release a few seconds later, and then the three of them went still as their minds slowly returned.

Luke's gaze met Kit's, and he saw the same adoration and awe on his brother's face that Kit felt in his heart. They had found the one they were meant to be with and made her their own. Their lives would never be the same again. She was theirs to love, cherish, and protect forever, and he knew they would both give up their lives for her.

She stirred between them as Luke withdrew. She drew in a slow, shuddering breath, and her eyes flew open. "Did I—"

"It would appear your Pheran side wasn't interested in waiting for an official ceremony," Kit confirmed, smiling as her skin darkened in her version of a blush.

"We're yours now," Luke added. He knelt on the bed beside them and leaned in to nuzzle her hair.

"For once, I'm in agreement with my blue half," she said, laughing and happy.

"How are you feeling?" Kit asked

"I'm fine. What parts of me I can still feel don't hurt at all." She grinned and kissed his cheek before glancing over at Luke and blowing him a kiss from her fingers.

"Good. In that case, my vote is we finish making the bed and then put it to good use for the next few hours."

She glanced around and nodded. "Sounds like a plan. Did you take all the bedding to make this thing?"

"We left a bed for your brother. He's going to need a place to sleep on the way home," Luke said.

Zura nodded slowly. "Thank you. I hope that's all he needs to recover from this nightmare."

"I checked the medical supplies before we left. We've got everything we need to take care any minor injuries once he's safely on board, and I have no doubt our friends will want to check him over before we head home. We're going to get him back, gorgeous. I promise."

There were tears in her eyes as she nodded again.

"I know. I'm glad you're both here…my *vardo*," she spoke the Pheran word for life mate for the first time.

Kit cupped her cheek in his hand and tried to find the words to tell her what was in his heart. "There is nowhere else in the universe we'd rather be. We spent years dreaming of the day we'd have a place to call home and someone special to share it with. Now you're in our lives, and there is nothing we wouldn't do for you."

"I love you both so much," she said softly. "Thank you."

CHAPTER THIRTEEN

Zura sat in the cockpit of the *Sun Sprite* and tried to keep her mind focused on the task at hand. She was only minutes away from docking, and she couldn't afford to let herself get distracted. This close to the end of the trip, it wasn't easy to think about anything but getting Royan back.

They'd gone over the plan countless times during the past few hours. Not that it was much of a plan. Vin's message had made it clear that she was to come alone, which meant that Luke and Kit would have to stay out of sight on the *Sun Sprite*. They still weren't happy about it, but they had grudgingly agreed once she made it clear that their appearance could put her brother's life at risk. She was going in armed, and they had made some modifications to her comm device so that it would broadcast both audio and visual signals back to the ship.

True to his word, instructions had been sent to the *Sun Sprite* shortly after she'd requested permission to dock. The meeting would happen shortly after landing, the location was confirmed at the Blast Zone. She had used the encrypted channel to update Dash and Mack, and they had responded immediately, confirming they were ready and waiting. If anything went wrong, they would move in, and she knew her *vardo* would be at her side the second they thought she was in danger.

Not that she believed Vin would try anything. She knew him too well. He would play things cool and reasonable because he believed he had the upper hand. As long as she let him believe he was in charge, things should go smoothly enough.

She guided the *Sun Sprite* into her assigned berth, wincing slightly as the ship made final contact with less than her usual finesse. If her father were alive, he would have mocked her for a week for making such a hard landing. Of course, if he were still alive, she wouldn't be in this mess in the first place. Her hand smacked down on the edge of the console as she gave vent to her frustration. *Damn it, Dad. Why didn't you tell me what you were up to?*

"I've never seen anyone spank a ship for a rough landing before," Luke drawled from the cockpit door.

"One more comment on my piloting skills and I'll spank *you*, big guy," she shot back as she unfastened her harness and pushed herself out of her chair.

"*Fraxx*, I love it when you get all riled and threaten violence. It's sexy as hell."

"You're insane. Most people run the other way when I get riled."

He grinned at her. "Their loss. Besides, you didn't pick a couple of wimpy, normal humans to fall for; you went for a pair of cyborgs. We don't run away from danger. We run toward it."

"Well, that explains how you ended up with me. Lately, I seem to be a danger magnet. My life was never dull, but it never used to be this bad. You sure you're not going to lose interest again once things get back to normal?" She was half-joking, but Luke didn't laugh. Instead, he hauled her up against his hard body and then spun her around until her back met the wall.

"I'm never going to lose interest in you. I love you, Zura. There will never be another woman who makes me feel the way you do. If you even *think* something is off at this meeting, you cut and run, do you hear me? If it comes down to a choice between your life or your brother's, you save yourself. If Royan is any kind of brother, that's the choice he'd want you to make."

"You don't know my brother at all. You can't know what he'd want," she argued. Not that she disagreed with him, but this wasn't a conversation she wanted to have right now.

"I know what I'd want if it were my sister. There is no way I'd want to live if it was at the cost of her life."

"It's my fault he's involved. If I had met with Vin when he wanted me to…"

"It's not your fault. This is all on Vin, and he's going to pay for it in blood. If you had gone to meet him, he would have taken your ship and done *fraxx* knows what to you. You didn't know about the ring yet. You had nothing to give him." Luke crushed her to him and kissed her hard. "You meet with him, tell him what he wants to hear, and come back to us as fast as you can."

"I will."

"You better. If not, we're coming after you," Kit said, joining them despite the crowded conditions.

She hadn't even heard him approach, but now he was pressed in tight behind her, his hand on her shoulder, his thumb gently stroking her neck. "I promise I'm not going to take any chances. My best chance of getting Royan back is to follow the plan we made. Don't worry, guys, you're not going to lose me."

"Damn right we're not," Luke said, his voice a low rumble.

"As much as I love it when you two get all protective and mushy, I really need to get going. We're on the clock, remember?" She leaned into Kit and closed her eyes, enjoying one last moment of closeness. Despite all her assurances, she knew there was a chance this would be the last time they were together. The thought made her heart ache.

It wouldn't be fair to finally have everything she dreamed of, only to have it end before it had really begun. Of course, she also knew that life was rarely fair. All she could do was be grateful for what time they had been given and hope like hell they all made it out of this mess in one piece.

"You sure you don't want us to come with you?" Kit asked again.

"Of course I want you to, but you can't. Vin's cocky, but unfortunately for us, he's also a distrustful bastard. He'll have someone watching the ship to see if I'm alone. You two need to stay out of sight and protect the *Sun Sprite* if anyone tries to mess with her while I'm gone." She turned to look at Kit. "Take good care of her. She's important to me."

"And you're important to us. Try to come back in the same condition you left," Luke said before kissing her temple and letting her go. Kit held her for a moment longer, but then he moved back, and she knew it was time to go.

"I'll be back soon. Then we'll go get my brother and end this nightmare. I love you both." She squeezed past Kit, pulled up the hood on her cloak, and didn't look back. They had already said everything that mattered.

Kit took a seat in the cockpit and activated the link to Zura's comm device. He followed her progress, and the moment she was off the ship, he locked the doors and activated the *Sun Sprite*'s security system. Protecting the ship was the least he could do for her, she was the one who was walking into a dangerous situation without him. He hated that he wasn't with her right now. He wasn't used to sitting on the sidelines when someone he cared about was in danger.

"Screw this, I'm going after her." He was halfway out of the chair when Luke's hand clapped down on his shoulder.

"No, you're not. Trust me, I hate this as much as you do, but we need to stay out of sight. This is the easy part, remember? She meets the asshole who took Royan, they arrange for an exchange, and she comes straight back here. We're her ace in the hole."

"We should be with her." Kit threw off his brother's hand and rose to his feet.

Luke planted his feet on the deck and faced him, his arms crossed over his chest. "Don't even think about it."

Kit slammed a hand into the chair. "You're really going to stop me? She claimed us as her *vardo*, Luke. She's ours forever."

"She is, and she can take care of herself. I have faith in her. If you go out there now, you're going to put her and her brother in jeopardy. Sit your ass back down and be patient. Our time is coming."

"I still hate this plan, but I'll stay put for now and take it out on Vin later." He met his brother's eyes. "We're in agreement that he's not going to survive long enough to wind up in custody?"

"No chance of that. If you don't kill him, I will."

With a brief nod of assent, Kit eased himself back into the pilot's chair and checked the monitor showing Zura's progress. She was walking through a crowd, and he grinned a little as he heard her muttering under her breath as she tried to push through the throng. Luke was right, their girl could take care of herself.

* * * *

Zura made it to the entrance to the Blast Zone without spotting any of the Corp-Sec personnel she knew were tracking her movements. They were damned good at avoiding notice, and that made it easier for her to relax. They were out there, watching over her right now, and they were her best chance of getting Royan back and making sure Vin never bothered her again.

She crossed the threshold and left the noisy clamor of the crowd behind her. Inside, conversations were hushed, the music was low, and the soft lighting allowed for a few shadowy corners without casting the entire place in darkness. Thick carpets covered the floor, muffling her footsteps as she moved through the place, looking for Vin.

She recognized a few of her fellow pilots seated around the place, most of them enjoying a drink or a meal with their shipmates. There were a handful of them studiously avoiding her gaze, and she made a mental note of who they were and where they were sitting. It was clear to her that they knew why she was here, and she had to assume they wouldn't be on her side if things went sideways.

Vin was waiting for her in the farthest corner, his back to the windows that lined the entire outer wall. Zura pretended not to see him at first. Instead, she made it appear she was distracted by the view outside while she took note of the exits and the location of anyone who might be one of Vin's crew. There were a few potential candidates, but it was impossible to know for sure. The only one she recognized was Ganzer, and he was sitting beside Vin. Beyond the two of them was the breathtaking vista that allowed the owners of the Blast Zone to charge such exorbitant prices without anyone complaining...much.

The far end of the Drift was close enough to the asteroid belt that you could see it with the naked eye. It was a thin ribbon of ever-changing colors and shapes as the massive rocks performed their eons old dance in the light of the system's slowly dying star.

Space vessels of every size and configuration came and went from view as they transferred cargo, ore, and personnel around the Drift and into the belt. It was a sight worth seeing, and one day, she would bring Kit and Luke here to see it with her.

Not today, though. Today she had business to attend to.

Satisfied that she had identified all the exits and potential problems in the immediate area, Zura let her gaze fall on Vin and made her way over to his table. He looked the same as ever. He wore his brown hair slicked back into a ponytail, and he flashed her a smile that reminded her of pictures she had seen of an extinct, predatory fish that had once swum in Earth's oceans.

"You're looking good, Zura. Made it with time to spare, too," he said by way of a greeting.

"When have you ever known me to miss a deadline?" she shot back, her nerves putting more bite in the retort than she had intended. She needed to be calm and clear-headed, but it was hard to do when faced with the bastard who had abused her and then kidnapped her brother to force her into this meeting.

Vin laughed, though there wasn't much humor in the sound. "You haven't changed a bit. Have a seat and we can catch up."

She chose to sit in the booth with them. Not that she wanted to be that close to him, but the chairs on the table side all left her with her back to the room, exposed. "We're not here to catch up, Vin. You have my brother, and I'm here to make a deal to get him back. I don't even know what it is you want, so how about we start with that. Why am I here, and what do you need from me?"

He clasped a hand to his chest. "You wound me, baby. There was a time when we were a whole lot more than friends."

"That ship left orbit a long time ago. You know the reasons why I left; there's no reason to rehash the past. I'd rather talk about the present." She tapped her index finger against the tabletop. "Why the *fraxx* are we having this meeting at all?"

He frowned and for a moment his masked slipped, showing her the dark, dangerous man behind the smile. "It doesn't have to be this way, Zura. I've got a good thing going these days. You could be part of it."

She choked back a horrified laugh. "That's never going to happen. Even if we set aside everything you did to me, you still kidnapped my brother and beat the hell out of him to make me meet with you. I'm here to get him back, and that's all I'm here for."

"The business with Royan is your fault. If you had come to meet with me when I asked nicely, none of this would have been necessary. You make me crazy, baby. You always have. You shouldn't have left me like that. Then, when I finally found you again, you hide in a *fraxxing* fight club instead of meeting with me like I wanted. You're the one that made all this happen."

Zura ignored his comments. He always did that, making excuses and casting blame for his actions on others. She wanted to argue with him, to point out the holes in his logic, but there wasn't any point. He would only get angry, and that was the last thing she needed. Her best chance was to stay quiet and let him think he was holding all the cards. This wasn't about their past, it was about getting Royan back.

It was interesting to note that while he knew she was staying at the club, he didn't appear to know about her relationship with Kit and Luke. How ever he was getting his information, his source didn't know everything. At some point, she intended to find out who was ratting her out and make sure they paid for their part in all of this.

Instead of ripping into Vin or demanding answers she knew he wouldn't give her, she took a slow breath and looked him squarely in the eye. "I'm here now. That's all that should matter to you. I want Royan back, and I want him back alive and well and in one piece."

Vin scoffed and waved his hand. "Your brother's fine. Any damage we did to him was in self-defense. He didn't come quietly. Some of my men got their asses handed to them trying to take him down."

"Where is he?" she asked without letting him hear the relief she felt at hearing Royan was okay.

"Somewhere safe. You hand over the *Sun Sprite* and everything else your dad gave you and I'll take you to him. Once I find what I'm looking for, I'll cut you both loose."

It was time to play the only cards she had left. "I'm not keen on the idea of being your guest for any length of time. In fact, I'd rather skip that part of your plan. If you're after what I think you are, you don't need my ship. I have everything you want right here." She held out the chain with her father's ring hanging from the end.

"What's that piece of junk got to do with anything?" Vin's tone was dubious, but his gaze never strayed from the ring around her neck.

"Turns out Dad's ring is more than it appears. I recently discovered that the gem is a data crystal. He hid a video recording for me on it, along with a stash of cash. I assume the money is what you're after. It's all yours in exchange for Royan."

His eyes were nearly glowing with greed as he held out his hand to her and snapped his fingers. "Hand it over."

"Not a chance. This is my only bargaining chip. Did you really think I was going to hand it to you just like that?" She slipped the ring beneath her shirt again. She couldn't let him get his hands on the crystal until Royan was safe.

Vin shrugged, an indulgent sneer on his lips. "It was worth a try."

She lowered her gaze and softened her voice, trying to appear defeated. "You can have the money, Vin. Take the ring, too. Just give me my brother and it's all yours."

"What you lack in looks, you always did make up for in smarts," Vin said.

"I'm smart enough to know this place is full of your men. I want to do the exchange somewhere else, somewhere I can see what's coming at me."

"Works for me." He rattled off a set of coordinates for a location only a short hop from where they were currently located. "Take off as soon as you can and meet us there."

Zura nodded, her thoughts racing almost as fast as her pulse. She had expected him to name a location here on the Drift, not out in space. She couldn't decide if this was a good turn of events or not. "Will do."

Ganzer cleared his throat. "Vin? The chief didn't give the okay for us to bring anyone to the ship. You sure this is a good idea?"

Vin snarled and glared at Ganzer. "Of course I'm *fraxxing* sure. I don't need to ask permission for every little thing I do. I'm not a spineless wimp like you, I know how to take the initiative and get things done. There's nowhere around here that isn't under surveillance. I'm taking this exchange somewhere quiet where we can do our business without interruption. You got a problem with that?"

The Jeskyran blanched, not a good look for someone with his yellowish coloring. "Whatever you say, boss."

"That's right. I am your boss. Don't *fraxxing* forget it again or you'll be sucking vacuum."

Zura watched the drama play out without saying a word or even changing her expression, but it wasn't easy. Seeing Vin lose his temper reminded her of the last time they'd been together. That had been the night she had confronted him about the thefts, the cheating, and his lies. That was the first, last, and only time he had beaten her. The second she was released from medical, she had taken the *Sun Sprite* and left. The moment Royan learned what had happened, he'd met up with her and hadn't left her alone until they were both convinced she was safe. He'd been there for her, and now she was going to do the same for him.

"We done here? I believe we both have somewhere else to be soon, and I'd like to get going," she asked.

Vin nodded. "One more thing, Zura. When I get to the rendezvous, if I see so much as a piece of space junk floating where it shouldn't be, your brother is a dead man. You've been smart so far, following instructions and keeping things just between us. Keep it up and this will all be over soon."

She shrugged and let her head sag forward a little. "You're holding all the cards, Vin. I get that. You deliver Royan to me, and you'll get what you want."

"Good girl. I'll see you soon." Vin drained the rest of his drink and then wiped his mouth with the back of his hand.

Aware she had been summarily dismissed, Zura rose from the table in silence and made her way back to the same door she had come in. Once she was outside, she exhaled harshly and headed straight for the *Sun Sprite*.

"I'm coming back now. I'm okay," she muttered just loudly enough for her comm device to pick up her words and broadcast them to Kit and Luke. She couldn't risk anything more than a brief message. Vin would have men watching her, and she couldn't give them any reason to think she wasn't going along with his plan.

Back on the *Sun Sprite*, Luke sighed in relief as her message came through. "Thank *fraxx* she's out of there. Killing that son of a bitch is going to be a pleasure."

"Agreed." Kit rolled his shoulders and then twisted in his seat to look at Luke. "I don't like the fact the next rendezvous is going to be out there. It's going to make it harder for Mack and Dash to avoid being spotted."

Luke nodded. "I don't like it either, but it's not like we have a choice. Besides, when have you ever known a plan to survive contact with the enemy?"

His brother ran a hand through his hair and grunted in acknowledgment. "That's the truth. I thought we'd left these days behind us when we left service. I was enjoying retirement."

"Me, too. Hopefully, we can go back to busting heads back at the Nova after this. Maybe after we take Zura to bed and don't come out of our quarters for a week."

"Make it two weeks and you've got yourself a plan."

Both of them lapsed into silence again as they tracked Zura's progress across the station. The moment she was safely on board, they left the cockpit to join her. Luke knew he wouldn't truly relax until he had her in his arms again.

She stomped down the main corridor toward them. "I hate that slimy jerk. What the hell did I ever see in him? Once we have Royan back, I hope you two tear him to pieces. Slowly. Tell me you heard everything and you've already sent a message to your friends telling them about the change in plans."

"Damn. Has anyone told you that you are glorious when you're pissed?" Luke asked as he intercepted her and drew her into his arms. She glowered at him for a moment, then broke into laughter as she burrowed into his arms.

"Only the two of you are crazy enough to think so. So, did you catch the coordinates for our next meeting?"

Kit nodded. "We heard. We sent out an encrypted message right away and got an acknowledgment back. They're already on the move."

"We need to be moving, too. Vin didn't give me much time. I guess he thinks it will reduce the chances of me inviting anyone else to the party. He doesn't know me as well as he thinks he does."

"If he knew you at all, he would be on the fastest ship he could find and already be running to the far side of the cosmos," Kit agreed.

Luke didn't say a word. Instead, he dipped his head and kissed his beautiful, courageous love. He had no idea what the future held, but one thing he was certain of was that it would never be boring.

"You're getting ahead of yourself, Luke. First, we save my brother, then we celebrate."

"Yes, captain," he drawled, earning himself another grin.

"*Veth*, I love it when you two say that to me. Now, let go of me so I can start preparing for departure. Kit, do me a favor and run a check on all our defense systems. I have a feeling we're going to need them."

CHAPTER FOURTEEN

Kit checked the time again. They were waiting for an update from Mack and Dash, but so far there had been nothing but silence. He knew his friends were out there somewhere, but where? In a few short minutes, they would arrive at the coordinates Vin provided, and from what he could tell, it was an ideal place for an ambush. There was nothing out this way but empty space and asteroids, and plenty of places for a ship to hide.

The entire asteroid field was all that was left of two small planets that had once orbited the system's sun. Somewhere in the distant past, the two planets had collided, spawning a huge expanse of debris-strewn space. Vin and his buddies could take cover near any one of the tens of thousands of massive rocks that were scattered across the sector. Some of those asteroids were big enough to hide a *fraxxing* space cruiser.

Please, don't let them have anything that big or well-armed.

"I hate to be the first one to point out the obvious, but where the hell is everyone?" Luke said, gesturing to the monitors showing the empty asteroid belt outside.

"They're probably still trying to get all the pieces in place. We were all expecting the exchange to take place somewhere on the Drift," Zura said.

"Which is mostly likely why Vin opted to move it out here," Kit agreed.

Zura's comm device chimed. She scanned the incoming message, replied, and then blew out a harried breath. "Our backup is here, and they brought friends. There are three Corp-Sec ships in the vicinity. They're staying out of scanning range until we give them the signal to move in. All we have to do is go in, get Royan, and get our asses out of the line of fire before all hell breaks loose. Speaking of scanning range, it's time the two of you headed to the cargo bay."

"You sure they won't be able to detect our life signs if we're in there?" Luke asked.

"I'm positive. Dad had some…interesting modifications done to that part of the ship over the years. It can be completely shielded as needed, which was very handy when he was running black market merchandise."

"Your father wasn't exactly trying to be nominated for parent of the year, was he? I can't believe you were raised around all this and still managed to be a good, decent human being," Luke said, throwing his hands out to encompass the ship.

She laughed. "I'm only half human. Dad always said I took after my mother. Wait until you meet, Royan. He's just like our father."

"*Fraxx*, I just realized that this rescue is also going to be our first introduction to your family. I hope we make a good first impression," Kit said with a grin.

"You're charging in to save his ass. As first impressions go, I'd say that has to be a ten out of ten." Zura shooed them out of the cockpit and ordered the ship's computer to take over navigating before joining them in the corridor. She squeezed by them to take the lead on the way to the cargo bay while Kit took a moment to enjoy the view of her sexy curves from behind. He still couldn't believe she was all theirs. Beautiful. Brave. Full of life and fire.

Whatever it took to retrieve her brother and keep her safe, Kit would do it. He had spent his entire life as a soldier fighting in battles that had no meaning for him. This time was different. This time, he was fighting for his future and the future of the woman he loved.

* * * *

Zura was still seeing her *vardo* settled in the cargo bay when an alert sounded, letting her know the computer had detected another ship nearby.

"Go. We're good here. You can fill us in on what's going on over comms," Kit said, pointing toward the door.

"We'll see you soon. Don't start the fun without us," Luke added, blowing her a kiss.

"You're both crazy, but I love you. Thank you for coming with me," she told them before turning on her heel and jogging back to the cockpit.

The moment she could see the monitors, she uttered a curse and stopped dead in her tracks. "Holy hell. Who the *fraxx* are you working for these days, Vin?"

There was another ship out there all right, but it wasn't a shuttle or a small freighter like the one she'd expected. It was much bigger. From what she could see, it had been a commercial vessel at some point in its life, but even at first glance, she could see it had been modified, and whoever had done it hadn't cared about aesthetics. Its once streamlined form was now misshapen, and the formerly pristine white hull was marred with a patchwork of different paint jobs and parts. There were no identifying marks on it anywhere. Not even a name or a number.

The ship was large enough to dwarf the *Sun Sprite*. In fact, her entire ship could probably fit inside one of its hangars. The second the thought crossed her mind, she realized that was likely what was going to happen. She had expected a ship-to-ship docking to handle the exchange. Like most freighters, the *Sun Sprite*'s cargo bay had a sealed airlock that could be used to link up to another ship for the quick transfer of goods.

So much for Plan B. On to Plan C.

"Guys? I found our rendezvous point, and there is a huge *fraxxing* ship waiting for us already. I haven't heard from them yet, but it's big enough that I'm going to guess we'll be landing in one of their hangars and making the trade there."

"*Veth*. If we have to get out of there in a hurry, can you do it?" Luke asked over their comms.

"If we have to haul ass, Kit can blow the hangar door open, and I'll get us out. You two stay put for now. You can still come out the cargo bay door when the time comes. I'm going to let the others know what they'll be up against."

She captured an image of the other ship and sent it over her encrypted link to the ships standing by. The more information they had going in, the better the odds that everything went their way.

She settled back into her seat and took over manual control while she waited for the other ship to make contact. In the meantime, she studied the other craft. It was carefully synchronized with one of the larger asteroids so that the two of them tumbled together, which explained why her ship hadn't detected it until she was nearly on top of the damned thing. It was using the massive chunk of rock to mask its presence. If she hadn't been given these specific coordinates, she would've flown right by without ever knowing it was there.

Two minutes later she was finally hailed, and her heart started to pound. This was it. Showtime.

"Attention incoming vessel. Identify yourself," a cold voice demanded.

She flipped a switch on her console, activating the ship's communication system. "This is the cargo vessel *Sun Sprite*. I believe you're expecting me."

There was a brief pause, and then the chilly male voice was back. "Confirmed. You are instructed to dock in hangar two at the aft of the ship. Make your approach slowly and do not alter course or you will be fired upon."

"Setting course now," she answered tersely before deactivating the mic. "Real warm and fuzzy welcome there. I hope that hangar is clearly marked or this is going to be tricky."

Once the course was set, she activated her comm device and spoke to her *vardo*. "I was right. We're landing inside the other ship, which should tell you how big it is. There's been no word from Vin yet, but they were expecting us, so he has to be close by. He's probably on board already. I didn't exactly tax the engines getting here. I hope Royan forgives me for that."

"You gave our Corp-Sec buddies the time they needed to get everything in place. He'll understand. You came for him. That's all that matters," Kit said.

His words soothed her nerves a little, and she smiled to herself. "Thanks. I'm going to switch my comm device over to broadcast mode now. I'll see you both after we land. I trust you to know when to make an appearance."

"We wouldn't miss this for anything, gorgeous. See you soon," Luke added before both of them went silent again.

The rest of the flight passed quickly. A few simple maneuvers to line up with the only open hangar door, and then a straightforward landing. Less than three seconds after she cleared the hangar doors, they started to close behind her. By the time the *Sun Sprite* touched down, the doors were sealed, and atmosphere was already filling the hangar. She stayed seated, waiting for her next instructions. It didn't take long before the voice was back.

"You will exit your ship via the main door. No weapons. Walk forward thirty paces and then halt. You will be met, and further instructions will be given."

"Acknowledged," she replied and then headed for the door, aware that her *vardo* had heard every word.

She waited at the door until the computer indicated that there was sufficient atmosphere for her to breathe normally. As the door slid open, a ramp extruded from the ship, providing her with an easy descent to the hangar floor. The hangar itself was empty apart from the *Sun Sprite*. The walls were bare, and the floor had only a few landing marks and lines that were so badly scratched and faded that she could barely recognize them for what they were. Whatever this ship was, it saw a lot of traffic.

She had only taken a couple of steps before a door opened on the far side of the space and a half-dozen grim-faced and well-armed men came through. She recognized Vin right away, but it was the sight of her brother being supported between two of the biggest guys that held her attention. Royan was on his feet, but just barely. His hands were bound in front of him, and he walked with an unsteady, halting gait that made her stomach twist.

"Royan!" She called his name, not caring what the others thought of her outburst.

His head came up at the sound of his name. One eye was completely swollen shut now, and there were more bruises on his face than she remembered seeing in the recording she had been sent. Anger tore through her, raw and red. The bastards were going to pay for every mark and bruise they'd given him.

"Ease up, baby. You can talk to Royan after you give me what I want." Vin continued walking toward her, but at a gesture from him, the others came to a halt.

Royan swayed between his guards but managed to stay upright by what looked to be sheer will. Zura's heart ached at the sight, and she swore that she would make this up to him somehow.

"You're not getting anything until I hear from him that he's okay," she retorted.

"Fine. Hey, loser. Tell your sister you're good so we can get on with this."

Royan looked straight at her and gave her a lopsided smile. "Hey, sis. I'm good. Seriously. You should see the other guys."

"Don't remind me what you cost me in men, asshole. You put three of my guys in the infirmary!"

"And one in the morgue," Royan said, then grunted as one of his guards slammed a fist into his side.

"Your brother has the Watson family charm. It's going to get him killed one of these days, just like your old man. I swear you're the only smart one in your whole family, Zura." Vin came to a stop less than two feet away from her and held out his hand. "Prove to me how smart you are and hand over the ring."

She unfastened the necklace and handed it to him, chain, ring, and all. "Here. Take it and give me Royan."

Vin cradled the ring in his hand like it was more precious than platinum. "Not yet. Once I've confirmed what this is, then you can go if you still want to. I brought you out here for a reason. I wanted you to see what your future could look like if you stuck with me. All this belongs to the people

I work for now. They're powerful, and they want a piece of the action out here. I'm offering you a chance to be part of something big."

She shook her head. "I don't want any part of you or whatever you're into this time."

He sighed. "You don't know what you're walking away from. Someday soon, you're going to regret saying no to me. Soon we're going to be the ones in control of the pharma trade out here, not the corporations."

"I doubt that. Are we done here? I want to get Royan out of here."

"Almost. Like I said, I need to confirm what's on this thing and make sure you aren't cheating me. If I like what I find, then you can go. If not, well….We need ships for our new venture. I'd prefer to take you and the *Sun Sprite* as a package deal, but if you're not interested, you better hope there's enough money here to make me happy. Otherwise, I'm keeping your ship, too."

"You bastard. We had a deal!" Zura yelled, feigning surprise. Of course the weasel was changing the rules; he thought he had her at a disadvantage.

He was so very wrong about that.

Kit was standing with his hand over the door panel, waiting for the right moment. When Vin changed the deal, he knew the time had come. He slapped his palm down on the pad and charged the still-opening door with Luke right behind him.

Fighting was what they had been created to do, and they were damned good at it. Cyborgs were a lethal blend of technology and biology, manufactured to be faster, stronger, and far more lethal than a normal human could ever be. Before he had taken more than a few strides, he knew the location of every enemy, their armament, and threat level. For the first time in his life, Kit was fighting a true enemy, one who didn't deserve a moment's mercy. This wasn't some faceless cyborg soldier or a drunken miner looking for a way to vent his frustration, this was the man who had hurt Zura and taken her brother hostage. Vin Collins was going to die for what he had done.

"You backstabbing bitch!" Vin bellowed as he spotted Luke and Kit charging out of the *Sun Sprite*'s cargo bay doors. He reached for Zura, who laughed at him as she danced out of his reach.

"Did you really think I would come out here alone? I knew you'd pull something like this," she said before darting past him to head straight for her brother and the two men guarding him.

"I've got Zura. You deal with Vin," Luke called out as he changed direction to go after her.

Kit tightened the grip on his knife as he closed the distance between himself and Vin. Vin might be large and well-muscled for a human, but he was no match for an enraged cyborg. He seemed to know it too, because the moment he saw Kit coming for him, Vin's eyes widened and he turned to flee. He didn't get very far.

A downward slash of his blade sliced Vin's shoulder wide open, and the man screamed in pain and stumbled. Instead of letting him fall, Kit caught Vin by the shoulder and spun him around so they were face to face. Another downward slash tore through the tendons in Vin's right arm, making him drop the weapon he had been about to fire.

"Who the *fraxx* are you?! Whatever she's paying you, I'll double it. No, triple!" Vin demanded through gritted teeth, every word slurred by pain and fear.

"I'm Zura's *vardo*, and there isn't enough scrip in the galaxy to buy your way out of this," Kit said and shook Vin like a rag doll.

"*Vardo*? She's mated to one of you?"

"Two of us, actually. I won the coin toss, so I get to be the one to kill you."

Vin sneered and managed to wrench himself free of Kit's grasp. "I don't *fraxxing* think so. You three against all of us? Do you have any idea where you are right now? You're standing on the deck of a Drojo Cartel ship. Look around you, buddy, because this is where you're going to die."

Kit lunged and slashed Vin across the chest, then stepped in and slammed his fist into the other man's jaw, snapping his head back so hard Vin's teeth clacked together.

"Who said we came alone?" Kit asked.

Right on cue, alarms rang out, echoing through the hangar bay at ear-shattering volume. "You have to love allies with impeccable timing, don't you agree? That would be Corp-Sec making their presence known."

"*Fraxx!*" Vin muttered through bloodied lips, his earlier bravado gone. "My employers are going to kill me for this."

"You're partially right. You're going to die now, but your bosses aren't the ones who are going to kill you." Kit finally gave in to his bloodlust and put an end to the man who had threatened the woman he loved. He slashed Vin's throat and watched with satisfaction as the other man collapsed to the floor and expired in a pool of his own blood.

He glanced up from the wreckage at his feet to look for Zura and Luke. His fiancée was standing beside her brother, both of them armed and watching the door. Luke was finishing off the remains of Vin's crew. When the last man crumpled to the deck, all three of them turned and started toward the *Sun Sprite*.

"Time to go! I think we've overstayed our welcome," Luke called out as he and Zura flanked Royan and helped him across the hangar.

Kit lingered for a moment to retrieve Zura's ring. He sheathed the knife and pulled out his blaster. Armed and ready, he ran over to help, taking Zura's place at Royan's side. "You run ahead and get the *Sun Sprite* ready to go, little one. We'll get your brother on board."

She nodded. "On it. Don't think this means I'm going to start letting you boss me around, though. I'm still the *fraxxing* captain."

She was gone before he could do more than chuckle. Damn, he loved her, sass, fire and all.

"Our fiancée is crazy. I swear she was ready to take them all on by herself," Luke muttered as they watched her run to the ship.

"Fiancée? Whoa. My sister is with you two? When did this happen?" Royan demanded.

"On the way here. We'd be at the Nova Club celebrating right now, but we had to come out here and rescue you instead."

"So long as I didn't miss the party. By the way, thanks for the rescue. At some point, I'm hoping someone explains what the *fraxx* this was all about. All I know is Vin is an asshole with an unhealthy obsession with my sister."

"Was an asshole, past tense," Kit said, jerking his head toward Vin's mangled body.

Royan glanced over and grunted in approval. "Good. You saved me the trouble of tracking him down later."

"Anything for family," Luke said, and all three men laughed.

That was the moment it all went to hell.

The alarms were still screaming, masking the sound of the doors opening behind them. The first any of them knew of the new arrivals was when the air around them exploded with weapon fire.

One of the shots caught Zura seconds before she made it to safety. Kit watched it happen, the scene playing out in some kind of terrible slow motion. He saw the bolt slam into her back, and he swore he could hear the sickening sizzle as it burned through her flight suit and into her skin. She staggered forward a half step and then dropped to her knees at the top of the ramp. Somehow she managed to keep going, her progress slowed to a painful crawl as she dragged herself onto the ship and out of danger.

They lifted Royan between them and charged the last few feet to the ship, taking sporadic fire every step of the way. The moment he hit the door, Kit took cover and started returning fire.

There were only three attackers. The rest were likely responding to the far greater threat of the Corp-Sec ships bearing down on them right now. He took them down quickly, grateful there weren't more. It wasn't until the last one fell that he felt a burning pain in his leg. One of the bastards had managed to graze him on their run back to the *Sun Sprite*. He switched off neural feedback from the injured area to kill the pain and kept going.

Luke swore his heart stopped beating the second he saw Zura go down. It didn't start again until he hurtled through the door and saw her struggling to sit up. She was alive.

Dropping into a crouch at her side, he placed a hand on her shoulder to stop her from trying to move again. "How bad is it?"

"Bad," she answered through gritted teeth and then looked past Luke to her brother. "Royan, you're going to have to get us out of here, the *Sun Sprite*'s all yours."

"You got it," Royan replied, looking down at Zura with worried eyes. "I promise I'll take good care of her."

"You better," she said and gave them a weak smile before letting her eyes close.

Royan and Kit worked their way past and headed for the cockpit. Luke noticed his brother's leg was bleeding slightly, but it looked minor enough. Kit's medi-bots would deal with the injury. Right now, Zura was the one he was worried about.

"I need to get you to medical so I can take a look at your injury. Hang in there." He carefully lifted her into his arms and got to his feet. Even though he was as gentle as he could be, she moaned in pain at being moved. He quickly realized that her clothing was soaked with blood, and so was the floor where she had been lying. He didn't need to be a doctor to know that he needed to get the bleeding stopped quickly, or they were going to lose her.

He headed toward the ship's small medical center as the engines came online. "Not much longer, now. We'll be home before you know it."

Zura nodded in response, but didn't open her eyes. By the time he got her there, her skin was pale; the moment he placed her on the bed, the medical scanner started to chirp, beeping alerts and warnings. Low blood pressure, poor oxygen levels, extensive tissue damage, he took it all in with a sinking feeling in his stomach. She was in bad shape, and this small medical bay wasn't equipped to handle injuries this serious. He injected her with healing accelerant and applied a blood clotting agent to the wound to try and slow the bleeding, but nothing seemed to help. They needed to get her to one of the other ships, fast.

"Zura, open your eyes. You need to stay awake."

She moaned and opened her eyes. "It's s'okay, Doesn't hurt anymore. Good drugs, thanks."

He couldn't bring himself to tell her he hadn't given her anything, yet. "That's good. You're going to be okay. You just lie still and let me take care of you."

He activated the internal comm channel he shared with Kit. *"She's in bad shape. We need to get her to a real doctor soon, or we're going to lose her. Tell Royan to haul ass to whichever friendly ship he sees first and let them know to have a medical team on standby."*

Kit responded almost instantly. *"Message relayed. Listen, you're going to want to hang on back there. Things are about to get bumpy. We're going to have to blast our way through the hungar doors."*

Luke barely had time to lean over Zura and grab the sides of the bed beneath her before the first salvo launched. He held on, keeping them both in place while the ship bucked and rocked.

When the muffled booms and blast waves finally ended, there were only a few seconds delay before the engines rose to a roar and they were moving.

"Going too fast, Royan. Quit showing off," Zura muttered softly before lapsing into silence again.

"Zura, you've got to stay awake right now. Royan's piloting, remember? Do you really want him flying your ship while you nap?"

"Tired," she murmured, but her eyes fluttered open again. "Who let him drive?"

"You did. You got shot rescuing him. Remember?'

She looked at him with confusion. "No…maybe? I remember Vin. Was a fight." Her eyes closed again. "Cold in here."

Luke wanted to scream in protest, to rage against what was happening. This wasn't how their story was supposed to end. He had to do something to save her. He brushed his lips against her cool cheek and whispered, "I'll get you another blanket. Be right back."

He grabbed a blanket out of one of the cubbies and tucked it around her while he activated his internal comm channel again. *"Kit, get down here. Now. We're losing her, and there's nothing I can do to stop it."*

"We're taking fire, but the shields are holding. It won't be much longer now."

"You don't understand. There's only one way we might be able to save her, and I don't know if it will even work."

There was a pause before Kit asked, *"There's no other way?"*

"None. Hurry. We're nearly out of time."

"I'm on my way. Don't wait for me to get there."

Luke returned to Zura's side and gathered her into his arms so that she was curled against his chest. "I've got you, and I'm not letting you go. Do you hear me, Zura? You're not going anywhere."

She uttered a weak sound that might have been his name, but that was all. She was fading quickly now, and he knew they were out of time. He managed to keep one arm around Zura as he rummaged through the supplies until he found what he was looking for, a blood testing kit. He grabbed the auto-syringe and pressed it to the side of his neck, aiming for the carotid artery. He got it on the first try.

He held it in place until it chirped, announcing a full sample had been taken. He had no idea if it would be enough. He wasn't sure that this would work at all, but he had to try. He couldn't lose her. He wouldn't.

He transferred the vial of his blood to an injector and pressed it against her arm. Before he hit the button, he kissed her one last time. "I suspect this is going to hurt, love. I'm sorry for that, but it's the only way I can think of to save you. Don't you dare leave us, Zura."

He activated the injector and watched as the contents of the vial vanished into her body. His blood was filled with medi-bots, microscopic nanobots that were designed to keep him alive and combat ready, even when severely wounded. Every cyborg had them, but cyborg physiology wasn't the same as human, or Pheran for that matter. The odds were that her body would reject the invading tech, and if that happened, she'd die.

The last time Luke tried something like this, it hadn't ended well. They'd been in the middle of a battlefield, on a planet so remote it had no name, only a number. A plasma grenade had gone off close enough to injure them all, but Dana was hit the worst. Cynder had cradled her sister in her arms, tears streaking through the dirt and ash on her cheeks as they had done all they could to save her. All they could do hadn't been enough. Not even transfusions of all of their medi-bots had been able to undo the terrible injuries Dana had suffered, and she had died, still held in Cynder's arms.

She was the last one to die before the Resource Wars ended and they had all been freed. Luke had hoped it would be the last death he would have to witness until he was an old man, but here he was again, holding the woman he loved as she fought for every breath.

When Kit arrived, he would add his medi-bots to the ones already coursing through Zura's bloodstream, and then they would have to wait.

If it worked, they'd know soon enough. If it didn't...Luke stopped his thoughts from going down that path. Zura had the heart of a warrior. He had to believe she would win this fight. Now that he had her in his life, he didn't know how to live without her. More than that, he didn't want to try.

CHAPTER FIFTEEN

Kit sat beside Zura's bedside and waited for her to wake up. He and Luke had taken turns staying with her since she had been hurt, only leaving long enough to eat, sleep, and return to her side once again. They were back home on Astek Station, and Zura was once again a patient in the medical center, only this time, she had company.

Her body hadn't rejected the medi-bots, but the differences between her body and a cyborg's meant that the healing process had taken a toll on her body. Her injuries were gone, but she had yet to regain consciousness. The doctors assured him that she would wake up when her body was ready, but it was killing him to see her lying so still and quiet. He needed to see her smile, hear her laugh, and tell him she was okay.

His own injury was already well healed, and Royan was recovering quickly as well. He was in the room next door and was making the medical staff crazy by constantly getting out of bed to check on his sister.

"How is she?" Luke asked in hushed tones as he slipped back into the room.

"The same. Why hasn't she woken up yet?" Kit rose from his chair to pace the small space around her bed.

Luke crossed over to the bed and leaned down to kiss her cheek. "Come on, gorgeous. It's time to wake up. You know Kit gets cranky when you make him wait."

"Like you're any better," Kit shot back.

"I'm not the one who snapped at that very nice Dr. Jefferies when she told you to be patient."

"It wasn't what she said, it was how she said it," Kit grumbled.

"Like she was a trained professional being asked the same question for the fiftieth time in one day?"

"You're an ass."

"Yep, but I'm a diplomatic ass. They still *like* me."

"Go fight somewhere else. I'm sleeping here," Zura muttered groggily.

Kit was at her side in a second. "No more sleeping, little one. You've slept enough already."

"Hey, gorgeous, welcome back."

She stirred and finally opened her beautiful silver eyes, and Kit felt the weight of the universe slip from his shoulders. She was going to be okay.

"Is Royan all right? Did we win? Where are we, and why do I feel like I got hit by a comet?" she asked, her voice a raspy croak.

"Yes, we won. Vin's dead, and everyone else on that other ship is either dead or in custody. You got shot in the back while we were rescuing your brother. He's fine. A little battered and bruised, but nothing serious. You're the one we've all been worried about," Kit said, taking her hand and holding it tight.

"We're back on Astek Station, in the medical center. Everyone's been asking about you. Even Cyn's been by every day to visit."

"Every day? How long was I out? And where's my ship?" Zura's mind wasn't as awake as her body, but things were slowly coming back to her.

"It felt like forever, but you were only out of it for a couple of days," Luke told her.

Kit chuckled. "I wondered how long it would take you to ask about the *Sun Sprite*. She's back at her berth, undergoing some minor repairs."

She sat up slowly. "So, my brother's okay, my ship is mostly okay, and you two are in one piece. Good. Next question: If I got shot, why aren't I in more pain? I ache, and my mouth feels like I've been eating cotton balls dipped in dust, but that's it."

Luke cleared his throat and looked at Kit. "You want to explain it, or shall I?"

"Explain what?" Zura demanded.

Kit cleared his throat. "You were dying, Zura. There was no way to get you to help in time, so we had to make a decision."

Her brain was still only working at half speed, but she didn't like the sound of that.

"What decision did you make?"

"We transferred some of the nanobots we carry to you. It's not exactly a standard procedure, but we couldn't think of anything else to do," Luke said.

"What does that mean, exactly?"

"It means that you've got millions of microscopic medi-bots in your body now. The doctors say there's no way to remove them. They're self-replicating, and apparently your body can handle their presence without rejecting them, which is almost unheard of. There was a lot of medical jargon involved in the explanations, but the short version is you're not likely to get sick again," Kit explained.

"Ever?" she asked, her mind reeling at the implications of what they'd just told her.

"Ever. The medi-bots will keep you healthy, heal you when you're injured, and uh… some other stuff." Luke rubbed the back of his neck and avoided looking at her.

She narrowed her eyes at Luke. "Care to explain what you mean by other stuff? Because I'm betting that it's something I'm going to want to know about."

"No one's sure what a cyborg's natural lifespan is. Most of us died in the wars, and the rest of us are still too young for there to be any data. All the experts know for sure is that we're going to live a long time, and we'll likely do it in perfect health. So…" Kit squeezed her hand again.

"So in theory, I'm going to live a long, very healthy life?" She exhaled sharply. Of all the news she had been expecting, perfect health and longevity weren't even on the list.

"We think so, yes. You okay with that?" Luke asked, swooping in to kiss her.

"You saved my life and made me quasi-immortal in the process. Why wouldn't I be okay with it?" Zura was still struggling to wrap her head around everything she had been told. Royan was safe. Her ship was okay. Her *vardo* were with her and she was infested with lifesaving microtech.

"In that case, it was all my idea. I love you, Zura. There isn't anything I wouldn't do to keep you with me," Luke said between kisses.

"I love you, too. You might want to wait until I've brushed my teeth before you kiss me, though. I must have serious morning breath."

"I don't care. I've been waiting ages for you to wake up. It hasn't been easy for any of us. Kit was ready to start breaking heads if you didn't wake up soon."

"I got discharged two days ago, but I wasn't leaving here without you," Kit confirmed.

"Discharged? Back up. You got hurt? When?"

"I got shot about thirty seconds after you did. It's only a graze, though. I'm fine, little one. I promise."

"If anything happened to you…" The thought made her heart ache. Kit and Luke had risked their lives to protect her and help rescue her brother. It was a gift without price, and she had no idea how to begin thanking them.

"We feel the same way about you," Luke said.

"I don't remember much about what happened. There was a fight, I was running back to the ship, and then it all goes blank."

"Trauma will do that. You got hit as you were heading through the door of the *Sun Sprite*. We found you on the deck just inside. Royan flew us out of there, and I got to blow a hole in the bay doors. If it wasn't for you getting hurt, the whole thing was kind of fun," Kit said.

She rolled her eyes. "Your definition of fun needs work. Is there a program I can upload to fix that?"

"Ha-ha. No. No messing with my software. Now, you're welcome to mess with my hardware anytime you'd like. The second you're released from this place, we have plans for you. Honeymoon type plans," Kit said, his eyes filling with heat.

"Oh hell no. No sexy talk in front of the brother, thanks very much." Royan appeared in the doorway and grinned at her. "Hey, sis. Nice of you to finally come back to us. These two have been climbing the walls waiting for you to quit the sleeping beauty routine. I still can't believe you took a pair of cyborgs as your *vardo*. Having spent a few days in their company, I can tell you that they're both crazy."

"Yeah, but they're my kind of crazy," Zura said, earning herself a wink from Kit.

"Damn right we are."

"I owe you an apology, Royan. I got you dragged into my mess, and I'm sorry."

Royan scoffed. "The way I hear it, we both got dragged into one of Dad's messes. Trust him to keep something like that a secret from us but manage to let Vin the asshole know about the money. You don't owe me anything. In fact, once you're out of here, I'm buying you a drink as thanks for coming to get me."

"Screw that. Drinks are on the house. You're family now, Royan. You don't pay for drinks in our club," Luke declared.

"Really? In that case, I might consider relocating to the Drift. Free booze for life!"

"Behave yourself, little brother or I'll have my *vardo* kick your ass." Zura sat up the rest of the way, then eased herself to the edge of the bed.

"Where do you think you're going?" Luke asked.

"Up. According to the two of you, I've been in bed for days. It's time I got back to my life."

She moved slowly, lowering herself to the floor a few inches at a time. No pain.

Good.

Once she was on her feet, she took a few cautious steps and found herself being tugged into Kit's arms.

"Come here, little one. There's something I need to return to you." He drew her in close and then held up her dad's lucky ring on its familiar gold chain.

"You got it back for me. Thank you," she said as he carefully fastened it around her neck.

"I had to. The first time you took the damned thing off you nearly died. It's your good luck charm, and we don't want you to ever take it off again."

It was funny, but she felt better for having the comforting weight of the ring back around her neck. For a fleeting moment, she wondered if her dad could see her right now and if he would approve of her choices. Somehow, she thought he would. The message he left for her said he hoped that she would find a better life for herself, and she had. She was with two men who loved her completely. Her brother was back in her life, which meant she had another chance to bridge the distance between them, and she had the gift of her father's money. For the first time in her life, she could do whatever she wanted, instead of what she had to.

"Zura? You okay? Do you need to go back to bed?" Kit asked, staring down at her with concern.

"I'll go back to bed in a minute. I'm okay, I guess it finally hit me that it's over. It is over, isn't it?"

"It's over. Vin's dead. Royan's safe. Corp-Sec is looking into the Drojo Cartel, which Vin mentioned was the name of the group who owned that big, ugly ship. We even know who was watching you. It turns out Vin was paying a couple of station crewmen to send updates whenever they saw you. They're all in custody now. Well, two are. Owen got a hold of the third one, he's in the secure section of the medical center, recovering. It's really over, Zura. It's time for us to go home." Kit told her.

Zura sighed happily and nestled into Kit's arms. "Home. I like the sound of that." She wasn't sure what her future would look like yet, but whatever she decided, Zura knew that from here on in, home wouldn't be the *Sun Sprite* anymore. It would be with her men and the family she had found here in the Drift.

* * * *

"You look amazing," Cyn told her as she finished zipping Zura into her dress.

"I barely recognize myself. You are a wonder with a make-up kit and a hairbrush, Cyn."

Cynder laughed. "Don't tell anyone, okay? That's our little secret."

"I won't tell a soul. I have to ask, why don't you ever…" Zura gestured to herself, and then to Cyn, who was dressed in her standard outfit of dark pants, a sleeveless Nova Club t-shirt that showed off her hard body, and combat boots. Her short hair was spiked up into gelled points, and as far as Zura could tell, she wasn't wearing any cosmetics.

Cyn shrugged. "I've had more than my share of male attention in my life already."

"I'm not surprised; you're beautiful."

The other woman laughed. "Thanks, but that's not what I meant. The corporations tinkered with a lot of behavior modifications over the years, but they quickly discovered that if they messed with our sex drive, it made the guys less aggressive in general. So instead of dialing it down, they dialed it up. Way up."

"So that's why Kit and Luke are, uh, the way they are?"

Cyn snickered. "Uh huh."

Zura already had an inkling where Cynder's explanation was going to lead, but she hoped Cyn would keep talking. Over the last two weeks, they had started to form a deeper friendship, and Zura wanted to know more about the woman she was coming to think of as family.

There was a long pause, and Cyn sighed. "You really want to hear this?"

"I want to know who you are, Cyn. So yes, I'd like to hear why you work so hard to keep men at a distance. I've gone my whole life feeling invisible and wishing someone would see me, so I know there's got to be a reason a beautiful woman like you is trying to hide."

"Because now I have a choice. Back then, I didn't. It took us years to overcome our conditioning and the behavior modification software those bastards installed in us. In the early years, I couldn't say no to any order I was given. Some of those orders included accommodating the sexual needs of my fellow cyborgs."

"That's horrible. I'm so sorry," Zura said. What else could she say? She couldn't imagine what Cyn had been through.

"Before you ask, no, I was never with your guys. For some reason, the corporation higher ups didn't like the idea of us having sex with our batch siblings. When we were fighting, there was no fraternizing, period. When we were back in barracks or being transported to a new location, that's when we were expected to make ourselves available."

"Now I understand why you don't want anyone to look at you that way."

"One day, maybe. But when I do, it will be my choice, you know? No one else's."

"I hope your one day comes soon, Cynder. You deserve to be happy and loved."

"You've certainly done that for Kit and Luke. I've never seen them so happy as they've been since the three of you finally got together." Cyn grinned. "You just keep doing what you're doing, little blue. You're good for them."

"They make me happy, too. I can't believe how much." Zura smoothed her hands over the long, cobalt blue and silver dress she had chosen to wear. They'd gotten married only a few hours ago in a small, private ceremony. Now, it was time for the reception. Everyone was invited, and from what she had heard, half the Drift planned on making an appearance at the club tonight.

"Come on; if we take any longer, my former commanders will be banging on the door demanding to know what we're doing in here. They hate having you out of their sight for very long."

Zura nodded. "I've noticed. I think they'll be even happier once they hear my news." Cyn had been the one person she had confided in about her plans. She loved her *vardo*, but she wanted this to be a surprise for them.

"Are you kidding me? They're going to be ecstatic. Come on. It's time we joined the party. You have an announcement to make."

They left Cyn's quarters together, passing Zura's new living quarters along the way. While the three of them were off rescuing Royan, Cyn had taken it upon herself to do a little remodeling. She had combined Kit and Luke's rooms, creating a larger space for the three of them. It was comfortable and far more spacious than anything

Zura was used to, and it was already starting to feel like home.

The moment she stepped through the doors, she was met with smiles and greetings from all directions. Before she could say more than a few hellos, a powerful pair of arms wrapped around her waist, and she was pulled back behind the bar.

"There you are, my bride. About time you got here," Luke said before spinning her around and sealing her mouth with a long, heated kiss that had several of the patrons cheering.

"Your sister was helping me get myself together. You like?" she asked when he finally lifted his lips from hers.

"I like. You look amazing. Of course, you're also going to look incredible when I get you out of that dress and make love to you all night."

"Sounds good to me," she replied. She reached up to brush her fingertips over the braided blue and silver metal band he now wore on his left hand. "Have I mentioned how sexy I think this is?"

He chuckled softly. "Not in a few hours, at least."

"Don't make me come back there and drag you to your own party. Put your bride down and get out here. You're not on duty tonight; you're supposed to be the guest of honor!" Cyn said, leaning on the far side of the bar with an amused expression.

"I'm not the only one working. Last time I saw Kit, he was headed to the front doors to check in with the two working security there."

Cyn threw her hands in the air. "I give up. Zura, they're all yours. Good luck."

"It's all a matter of incentive," Zura replied before lifting her comm device to her mouth and whispering something into it. Less than a minute later, Kit appeared through the crowd, his dark eyes gleaming as he made straight for her.

"What the hell did you tell him?" Luke asked.

Kit vaulted over the bar and pulled her into his arms. "No panties. Really? You're going to kill me, wife."

Cyn burst out laughing. "Nicely done, little blue."

"What? Did I miss something?" Kit asked as his hands cupped her ass, pulling her in close before kissing her.

"Not a thing," Cyn said with a slight snicker. "You ready, Zura?"

Zura held up a hand while she kissed Kit back with enough heat to make him groan deep in his chest. "Now, I'm ready."

"Ready for what?" Luke asked.

"You'll see."

Zura looked around at the throng of people that filled the bar. They were all here because they wanted to be part of the celebration. It was humbling to see so many familiar faces and to realize that they were all here for her and her *vardo*.

She had come out to the Drift because she had no other place to go, but somewhere along the way, it had become more than just a place to hide. It had become her home.

"Can you lift me onto the bar, please?" She asked her *vardo*.

"It's a good thing that's a long dress, or the answer would be no," Kit said before placing his hands on her hips and lifting her into the air. Luke moved in to help, and within seconds, she was standing on the bar top. Both men then moved around to the front of the bar, putting themselves between Zura and the crowd.

From here she could see every corner of the club, from the gaming tables to the booths in the far corners of the bar. There were friendly faces everywhere. Even a few of the medical staff were in attendance, including her doctor, Alyson Jefferies. Zura was still under medical supervision, and would be for some time to come. The doctor was writing a paper on Zura and her unique ability to survive the medi-bots that still coursed through her blood. So far, she was the only non-cyborg to survive such a transfer, and there were a lot of questions as to why and how.

Unofficially, the doctor wanted to know more about the cyborgs in general. The corporations guarded the facts about their creation and abilities so tightly that very little was known. With a number of the cyborgs calling the Drift home, Dr. Jefferies wanted to learn what she could about their unique physiology so they could turn to her for help, instead of the corporations that had created them.

Zura spotted Phyl seated in one of the booths and smiled at her. Phyl raised her drink and smiled back, clearly enjoying herself. The veteran pilot had shown up not long after Zura had been released from medical, and she seemed content to stay. She and Royan had become friends, too. In fact, they were getting along so well that it had started Zura thinking about not only her future but the future of the people she cared about.

She scanned the room until she spotted Royan. He had a drink in his hand and was chatting with Owen. The two of them had become fast friends in the last two weeks. He was staying at the club these days, and it was Zura's hope that he would soon agree to make the Drift his permanent home.

With everyone accounted for, she placed two fingers to her lips and let loose a piercing whistle that cut through the merrymaking. When all eyes were on her, she raised a hand and waved.

"I wanted to say thank you all for coming to celebrate with us tonight. As you know, I'm now married to Kit and Luke Armas, and I couldn't be happier!"

The cheers and applause took time to die down, but when it did, she continued speaking. "I have been welcomed into the Nova Club family with so much warmth, I cannot tell you what it means to me. For a long time, I thought I was alone. I believed that I would never have a family or call anywhere but the *Sun Sprite* home. Now I stand here with two men I love, surrounded by friends and family. There is nowhere else in the universe I would rather call home."

More applause rose, and she took the time to swallow down the lump in her throat. Without a word, Kit and Luke joined her on the bar, wrapping their arms around her in silent support. They didn't know what she was about to say, but they were there for her no matter what, and she loved them for it.

"I wanted all of you to be the first to know that I'm retiring as pilot of the *Sun Sprite*. I'm stepping aside so that my brother Royan can take over. Royan, you better take good care of my baby, or I will kick your ass from here to the edge of the galaxy."

Royan blinked in shock and then grinned. "You got it, sis."

There was more cheering, but she held up her hands to call for quiet. "I'm not done yet. Since I'm not captaining a ship anymore, I'll need a new job to keep me out of trouble. I've decided to open my own shipping business, bringing in rare and hard to find items for those of us on the Drift to enjoy. Royan, you're invited to be my first employee, and Phyl, you're welcome to join as well. I let both of you slip out of my life once before. I don't want to let that happen again.

"I'm proud of you," Kit whispered.

"So am I," Luke added, leaning down to kiss her cheek.

"I'm in!" Phyl announced in a loud voice. Zura already had a hunch Phyl would say yes once she heard the offer. Zura had done all she could to ensure that outcome by speaking to the veteran pilot at length about the future. Phyl was ready for a change, and this gave her a way to do it without surrendering her freedom.

"Me, too," Royan declared. "I think we need to raise our glasses to my sister. Congratulations on your marriage, your new business, and your new life. I wish you every happiness, Zura. You've earned it."

The entire bar erupted with cheers and well wishes, and Zura knew she had made the right decision. This was the right future, not just for her, but for all of them.

Kit couldn't stop grinning. Zura was staying on the station. They would have found a way to make it work if she wanted to keep running cargo, but this way they wouldn't have to. They could stay here and forge a life together. Not caring that they were still standing on the bar in front of everyone, Kit pulled Zura in close and kissed her with all the love and passion burning in his soul.

"I love you, little one. I'll love you from now until the last star burns out and the universe goes dark."

There were tears in her eyes as she smiled up at him. "I love you too. Both of you."

"You're sure you want to do this? Stay here on the Drift instead of being out there among the stars?" Luke asked.

"I'm sure. This is where I belong now. This is home. That doesn't mean I'm going to stay here forever. I'll still want to travel sometimes. Maybe see some of those planets I never got around to visiting. Take Luke to see a real ocean and lie on a warm beach somewhere. I always said I'd take a vacation someday when I could afford it. Now, I can, and I want my *vardo* to come with me."

Luke chuckled and stole Zura out of Kit's arms to kiss her. "You have yourself a deal," he told her softly. "You in, Kit?"

Kit nodded. It was more than time that they all took a vacation.

Raising his head, Luke bellowed his next words loud enough to be heard half a light-year away. "Zura's first act as the head of her own business is to declare that she's going on vacation, and we're going with her. Cynder, the club's all yours. We're going to the beach!"

Kit looked down at his beautiful wife as she stood wrapped in his brother's arms and thanked whatever forces in the universe had brought her into their lives. She was everything they dreamed of all their long, lonely years of service, and now she was theirs. Forever.

The End

ABOUT THE AUTHOR

Susan lives out on the Canadian west coast surrounded by open water, dear family, and good friends. She's jumped out of perfectly good airplanes on purpose and accidently swum with sharks on the Great Barrier Reef.

If the world ends, she plans to survive as the spunky, comedic sidekick to the heroes of the new world, because she's too damned short and out of shape to make it on her own for long.

To contact her about her books or to arrange end of the world team-ups, you can email her at *susan@susanhayes.ca.*

For all titles by Susan Hayes, please visit her website:
susanhayes.ca

To keep up with her latest news, releases, and appearances you can join her
Newsletter at:
http://eepurl.com/bd_GoH

www.ingramcontent.com/pod-product-compliance
Lightning Source LLC
Chambersburg PA
CBHW021001120726

47905CB00009B/2799